WINTER CARNIVAL

Elizabeth hung up in a daze. It was five-fifteen by now. The thought of Jeffrey standing at the intersection, watching hopefully as each car whizzed past, was heartbreaking. She would never forgive her sister for not getting the Fiat home on time. Never! Nothing Jessica had done in the past made any difference compared to this. Elizabeth felt as if she were going to explode with anger. She was certain she would never talk to her sister again.

And the way things were looking now, it appeared as though Jeffrey was never going to talk to her again. Elizabeth felt as if her entire world were collapsing, and all she could do was sit there and watch it crumble around her.

Bantam Books in the Sweet Valley High Series
Ask your bookseller for the books you have missed

SWEET VALLEY HIGH
Super Edition

WINTER CARNIVAL

Written by
Kate William

Created by
FRANCINE PASCAL

BANTAM BOOKS
TORONTO · NEW YORK · LONDON · SYDNEY · AUCKLAND

RL 6, IL age 12 and up

WINTER CARNIVAL
A Bantam Book / December 1986

Sweet Valley High is a trademark of Francine Pascal

Conceived by Francine Pascal

Produced by Cloverdale Press Inc.

Cover art by James Mathewuse

ISBN 0-553-26159-2

Published simultaneously in the United States and Canada

Bantam Books are published by Bantam Books, Inc. Its trademark, consisting of
the words "Bantam Books" and the portrayal of a rooster, is Registered in
U.S. Patent and Trademark Office and in other countries. Marca Registrada.
Bantam Books, Inc., 666 Fifth Avenue, New York, New York 10103.

PRINTED IN THE UNITED STATES OF AMERICA

O   0 9 8 7 6 5 4 3 2 1

WINTER CARNIVAL

One

It was four o'clock on a rainy Tuesday afternoon, and Elizabeth Wakefield was looking down at her sopping shoes, a rueful smile on her face. It figured that she'd miss the bus on one of the few rainy days they'd had all winter. And it also figured her twin sister, Jessica, would have taken the Fiat they shared to run an errand for the cheerleading squad. Elizabeth sighed. There were still four blocks to go before she got home, and at this rate she could practically swim!

Usually Elizabeth loved walking home; Sweet Valley was such a beautiful place. Its streets were lined with lush trees and colorful flowers that blossomed all year round, and there were occasional dazzling glimpses of the Pacific. But that afternoon Elizabeth would have preferred to be dry in the back of the school bus—or better still, in the driver's seat of the Fiat. If only Jessica had thought to ask her before—

Elizabeth squelched the disloyal thought before she could finish it. Jessica was Jessica, and that was all there was to it. Though she was only four minutes older than her identical twin, Elizabeth had always felt strangely protective of her. And she was annoyed with herself now for criticizing her sister's behavior, even to herself.

"I've just got the winter blues," Elizabeth said aloud, zipping up her jacket against the cool breeze and shifting her books to the other arm. She quickened her pace, lowering her head as she hurried into the wind. Elizabeth knew she didn't have anything to complain about. Winter in Sweet Valley was incredibly mild. On most days it was warm enough to go to the beach or sit outside by the pool in the Wakefields' backyard. And that particular winter, the weather had been even milder than usual. Both twins had been able to keep up their light golden tans.

2

Still, it seemed to Elizabeth that the midwinter blues were unavoidable, whatever the weather. And she had a bad case of them lately. It wasn't like Elizabeth not to be in the center of school activities, but for the past few weeks she had been feeling down. Not that anything specific was wrong. Elizabeth was a good student with a flair for writing. She was still working hard for *The Oracle*, the school newspaper. Roger Collins, the handsome young English teacher who was the faculty adviser to *The Oracle*, had encouraged Elizabeth to enter an essay contest several weeks before, and that had kept her busy as well. But her heart hadn't been in it. Her essay, titled ''Double or Nothing,'' was Elizabeth's attempt to describe how it felt to be a twin.

Maybe that was part of the trouble, she thought now, slowing down as she approached the Wakefields' pretty, split-level ranch house. It made Elizabeth feel terrible to admit it, but for the past few weeks, relations between her and Jessica had been slightly strained. Usually Elizabeth got a kick out of her sister's impetuous, slightly zany behavior. But lately it hadn't seemed like fun. In fact,

3

Jessica was starting to drive Elizabeth up a wall!

It struck Elizabeth now that part of the problem was that the twins always were expected to live up to the characteristics they were known for. People depended on those distinguishing character traits because the twins were mirror images—slim, five feet six, with sun-streaked blond hair tumbling to their shoulders and wide-set, aquamarine eyes. Close friends usually had no problem identifying them, though. Elizabeth dressed much more conservatively than Jessica, who usually looked like a model on the cover of the latest fashion magazine. She went through fads with so much enthusiasm and energy that Elizabeth sometimes couldn't believe she found time for everything else in her life. "Change" was Jessica's favorite word, whether it meant a new perfume, hairstyle, boyfriend, or hobby. "She's like a whirlwind!" Elizabeth had exclaimed once to Enid Rollins, her best friend.

"And you're so dependable," Enid had said loyally. Elizabeth sighed as she remembered that conversation. That was exactly what everyone always said about her—she was dependable. Loyal, steady, hardworking . . .

4

all complimentary terms, but hardly exciting. Elizabeth had always worked hard to live up to her reputation. She always met deadlines, both for homework and writing assignments for the newspaper. She was always on time and would never be caught without her wristwatch. She was considerate of her friends' feelings and tried to be a good listener, reminding herself that a writer had to be an observer of life. Listening to other people was the first step.

More often than not, Elizabeth had to cover for her twin, who considered traits such as dependability or promptness downright dull. Jessica lived by her own rules, relying on her charm—and her loyal sister—to get her out of the scrapes she invariably got herself into.

As she let herself into the house now with her key, Elizabeth found herself wishing that Jessica would be more considerate and more dependable. Take that afternoon, for instance. All Jessica had to do was ask her if she wanted a ride, instead of charging off with Amy Sutton to look for new pom-poms for the cheerleaders. Elizabeth grimaced as she kicked off her wet shoes. *I'm just being a brat*, she told herself, wandering in her stocking feet through the Wakefields' pretty front hall to the kitchen. She poured herself a glass of root beer and took a swallow, already relenting as she looked out at the rainy backyard.

It was just the time of the year that was getting her down, she thought. After all, she had everything going for her: a wonderful older brother, the best parents in the world, and her boyfriend, Jeffrey French, whom she felt incredibly close to.

And there were plenty of things to look forward to, she reminded herself. Everyone at school was getting excited about the big Winter Carnival coming up in a little over two weeks. The carnival was one of the biggest events of the year. An incredibly special weekend for juniors, seniors, and Sweet Valley High alumni, it was held at Mont Blanc, a ski resort located an hour and a half away from Sweet Valley. The year before, Elizabeth and Jessica had heard about the carnival from their older friends, and they had both been looking forward to this year, when they could participate themselves.

Elizabeth knew this year's carnival was going to be fantastic. And she was lucky that Jeffrey was looking forward to it as much as she was. The more she thought about the carnival, the more her spirits lifted. Her brother,

Steven, would take time off from college to attend the carnival, too, which would make it even more special. She had every reason to be excited about the whole thing!

Elizabeth was humming as she looked through the mail her mother had left on the counter in the kitchen. There was no mail for her that day. Elizabeth was disappointed. She and Enid had been eagerly waiting for the results of a contest they had entered. A local TV station was starting a brand-new trivia game show, which would star teenagers from the area pitting their trivia knowledge, team by team, against each other. As a public-relations gimmick, the TV station had run a contest for its initial contestants. One two-person team would be chosen from Sweet Valley High and one two-person team from Westwood High. The winners of the first round would appear on television in the first official trivia-show telecast.

Enid and Elizabeth were trivia buffs and knew they would have a good shot at winning if they were chosen. They were so enthusiastic about the idea that they had spent hours on their entry form, which consisted of ten sample trivia questions and an idea for the name of the new program. The selection was supposed to be made any day now. Since it was expected that there would be a number of correct entries, the final decision would be made by a drawing.

Elizabeth's reverie was shattered by the sound of the Fiat pulling up the front driveway. Jessica was home, and as usual her entrance was accompanied by an incredible clatter—doors slamming, books crashing to the floor, and an eager voice shouting, "I'm home!"

"I'm in the kitchen," Elizabeth called, smiling despite herself. She admired her twin's energy even as she found herself wishing Jessica would calm down every once in a while.

"Liz, you'll never believe in a million years—Amy just told me. I'm so excited! You know that trivia contest KSVC is running?" Jessica gasped, hurrying into the kitchen and opening the refrigerator door. "Mmm, cold lasagna," she added, prying off a lid from a Tupperware container. She got a fork, sat down at the table, and began to eat.

"What about the trivia show?" Elizabeth asked.

"I have to thank you, Liz. If it weren't for you, Amy and I never would have entered.

But when we saw you and Enid doing it, it looked kind of fun. We even swiped some of your answers. I hope you're not mad."

Elizabeth stared. She'd had no idea that Jessica and Amy had entered. She waited uneasily for Jessica to finish her story.

"Well, guess what? We won!" Jessica exclaimed triumphantly. "Isn't that great? Amy got the phone call while I was over there, and—"

"Don't tell me," Elizabeth said, her blue-green eyes narrowing. "You and Amy are going to be on the trivia show?"

Jessica nodded, thrilled. "Isn't that fantastic? They even want to call the show 'Trivia Bowl,' like we suggested."

Elizabeth felt her eyes fill with tears. It wasn't fair! Jessica and Amy couldn't have won—they just couldn't have!

"What's wrong?" Jessica asked, still gorging herself on lasagna.

"Nothing," Elizabeth lied. "It's just that Enid and I really wanted to be on that show. We worked so hard on our entry form, and—"

"Don't worry about it," Jessica advised her. "It's just a dumb trivia show. It's not such a big deal."

Elizabeth just stared at her. "But if *I'd* won

9

and you really wanted to be on it, I bet you'd twist my arm until I gave in and let you," she pointed out.

Jessica giggled. "I wouldn't do that," she protested. "Anyway, I couldn't swap with you even if I wanted to. Amy's really into it now. She's going to buy all these trivia books. She really wants to win so we can be on the first show."

Elizabeth bit her lip. She knew she was right. If the tables were turned, Jessica would get her way somehow. It was always like that. And Elizabeth always gave in.

The ironic thing was that Amy Sutton had once been Elizabeth's best friend—at least until Amy moved away from Sweet Valley. When she moved back recently, Elizabeth had been beside herself with joy. Unfortunately, Amy had changed a lot over the years, and Elizabeth finally realized that her former friend was much better suited to Jessica and her friends. These days she was too crazy about boys and clothing for Elizabeth's liking.

Now, Elizabeth felt that Amy had betrayed her. Sure, they had won the drawing. But only those contestants who had the right answers were eligible for the drawing. And Amy and Jessica wouldn't have had the right answers if they hadn't looked at her and Enid's entry. Elizabeth felt that Jessica was brushing it off too lightly. At the very least Jessica could *act* as if she felt sorry about it. As it was, Elizabeth thought she wasn't being terribly understanding.

Elizabeth was irritated about the whole thing. She was about to tell Jessica how she felt, but the phone rang, and her twin lunged toward it. "Hi, Amy!" she sang out happily. Elizabeth sighed and dragged herself out of the kitchen and up the stairs.

So much for the trivia show, she thought unhappily. It looked as if the midwinter blues were here to stay.

Two

"Hey," Enid said, pushing her tray back and eyeing her best friend with concern. "You haven't heard a word I've said."

Elizabeth sighed and stared down at her uneaten sandwich. "I'm sorry," she said unhappily. "I guess I've just got a lot on my mind, Enid. You were talking about the Winter Carnival, right?"

Enid smiled sympathetically. "That's all I've been talking about lately," she conceded apologetically. "I don't mean to be a bore, Liz. I'm just so wrapped up in the whole thing because of being co-chairperson of the dance committee."

"Enid, *I'm* the one who ought to apologize," Elizabeth said sincerely. "You're absolutely right to be excited about the dance! It's practically the biggest part of the whole weekend."

Enid giggled. "Guess what Winston wants to call it?" she asked, her green eyes sparkling. Winston Egbert, the acknowledged clown of the junior class, was Enid's co-chairperson. The dance was the highlight of the carnival and was traditionally held on Saturday night in the ballroom of the Mont Blanc Inn. Elizabeth knew Enid and Winston had been planning the dance for the last week or two.

Elizabeth thought for a minute. "Something silly, I bet."

"The Snow Ball," Enid said and giggled again. "Leave it to Winston, right?"

Elizabeth couldn't help laughing with Enid. "Don't tell me—are we going to have to dress like snowmen or something?"

"Huh-uh. Winston had all sorts of weird ideas, which I vetoed. But he insists on keeping the name."

As Elizabeth took a small bite of her sandwich, she tried to imagine what the weekend would be like. It sounded like a lot of fun. Cars and buses would leave from the school park-

13

ing lot early Friday afternoon, and Friday night the festivities would begin with an opening party at which Ms. Nora Dalton, the pretty young French teacher, and Mr. Collins would officiate. Quite a few of the teachers had signed up to be chaperons, and the arrangements at the inn had been made—four students to each room. Elizabeth would be rooming with Enid, Olivia Davidson, and Regina Morrow, and she knew the four of them would have a lot of fun together. Olivia was the shy, lovely arts editor of *The Oracle*. She had a great sense of humor beneath her reserve, and Elizabeth was sure she would be a fun weekend roommate. Regina Morrow had always been a special friend. Very beautiful, with her raven-black hair and huge blue eyes, she had been discovered by a local modeling agency and had won a coveted opportunity to be a cover girl for an issue of *Ingenue* magazine. Regina had spent some time in Switzerland, but now she was back in Sweet Valley, and the Winter Carnival weekend would be all the more special with her around to share in the fun.

It sounded as if the weekend was going to be action packed. Amy Sutton was organizing a miniature ice show that would take place on the rink outside the inn on Saturday afternoon. Two star athletes from the junior class—Ken Matthews, the blond captain of the football team, and Bill Chase, who had won medals as both a surfer and a swimmer—were setting up a mock winter olympics, which was going to run all day Saturday and Sunday. The students would be divided into four teams when they arrived at Mont Blanc, and their activities would be judged and awarded points, either on an individual or team basis. At the end of the weekend one team would be announced the winner. But there would be indoor events as well; for anyone who did not enjoy outdoor winter sports, the lodge would supply card and board games, Ping-Pong, and of course a good stock of steaming spiced cider and hot cocoa.

"It's going to be so much fun," Enid said happily as she finished her salad. "I think it's what we all need," she added, looking closely at Elizabeth. "It's always good to have a break in the middle of winter."

"Mmmm," Elizabeth said thoughtfully. She was looking forward to the carnival, too. But it was posing some problems. "Enid, what time does the opening party start on Friday night?"

"I think about seven. It's going to be a pizza

15

party, I think. Mr. Collins doesn't want it to last too late because he thinks we'll all be exhausted, and he wants everyone to be ready for the big day on Saturday."

Elizabeth looked upset. "Seven . . ." she murmured. She had been afraid of this. "Enid," she asked ruefully, "what have I done to get so unlucky all of a sudden?"

"What do you mean, unlucky?" Enid asked. "You're not still upset about the trivia show, are you?"

"A little," Elizabeth replied. "I mean, I wouldn't be upset if we'd lost fair and square. But it seems kind of rotten for Amy and Jessica to get on the show when they stole some of our answers and didn't even really care that much about it until a few days before the deadline. When I think about all the time we spent on those silly questions—"

"Well, it's annoying," Enid agreed, "but I don't think it qualifies you for being jinxed." She took a sip of her milk. "Is anything else wrong?"

"Well, it looks as if I'm going to have a hard time making the opening party of the carnival," Elizabeth said, frowning. "And I really hate to miss it. I know it'll be fun, and Jeffrey's going to be disappointed."

"What's the problem?"

"Todd called last night," Elizabeth told her, crumpling up her lunch bag. "You remember he's coming in for the carnival, right?"

Enid nodded. Todd Wilkins had been Elizabeth's steady boyfriend for a long time before his father's company transferred the family to Vermont. For a while the couple had tried to maintain the relationship despite the distance, but eventually they realized it wouldn't work. Elizabeth had been surprised to discover she didn't mind that much when Todd fell in love with someone else. But it had been a long time before she felt anything for another guy. Jeffrey French was the first.

When Jeffrey's family moved to Sweet Valley from Oregon, the blond junior had attracted a lot of attention. Jessica's good friend Lila Fowler, developed an instant crush on him and proceeded to do everything in her power to get him to reciprocate her feelings. At the same time, Elizabeth had been trying to act as matchmaker for Enid and Jeffrey. She smiled now, remembering what a failure her attempt at matchmaking had been. She'd been such a dope that she hadn't even realized that Jeffrey wasn't interested in Enid or Lila but in *her*.

17

That was all history. She and Jeffrey were serious about each other. They had wonderful times together, and Elizabeth trusted him with all her heart, and she knew he trusted her, too.

But they hadn't had to confront the problem of Todd yet. Jeffrey knew that Elizabeth and Todd kept in touch, but she had always had a suspicion that Jeffrey wasn't that crazy about the idea. Sometimes Elizabeth wondered if that could be traced to the fact that Jeffrey hadn't had a serious girlfriend before. There was no girl in his life who could compare to Todd in hers. If he occasionally seemed possessive of her or irrational about her friendship with Todd, Elizabeth attributed it to that.

All the same, Elizabeth felt uneasy about the prospect of the two boys meeting. And Todd's phone call hadn't helped ease her anxiety. "Remember that awards banquet he wanted us both to go to?" she asked Enid now. When Todd lived in Sweet Valley he had been involved with a program in which teenagers volunteered to be "big brothers" to underprivileged boys in the area. Todd had been assigned to a boy named Timothy Bryce. Even though Todd had moved, he and Timothy still kept in touch. They wrote each other letters and were very close. Todd had had quite an impact on the sixth grader's life, and Timothy looked up to him—and depended on him. Timothy had won a scholarship to a basketball camp, and the PTA was holding a dinner for award winners. The PTA wanted Todd to be present, and since the dinner coincided with the carnival, it offered Todd a double reason to return to Sweet Valley. He had asked Elizabeth to go with him to the dinner. Elizabeth had been looking forward to it.

"You told me," Enid said. "But isn't that Sunday evening after the carnival's over?"

Elizabeth shook her head. "That's what Todd thought the last time he called. But he just found out it's going to be Friday night instead. I guess at this point I really can't get out of it, but I know Jeffrey's going to be upset." She frowned again. "I haven't even told him about it yet," she admitted. "He got kind of upset when I mentioned Todd was going to the carnival, so I thought I'd wait till I knew for sure when the banquet was going to be held."

Enid looked sympathetic. "Sounds like things are kind of tense," she said. "It's funny. Jeffrey seems like he'd be so reasonable about things like that. I'd never have guessed he would turn out to be the jealous type."

"I know. It's kind of worrying me," Elizabeth responded. "In fact—" She broke off, seeing Jessica, Amy, and Lila Fowler coming over with their trays. "I'll tell you more later," she whispered, and Enid nodded.

Elizabeth didn't feel like sharing her concerns with Jessica and her friends, but she couldn't suppress her worry, either. And from the gleeful looks on the faces of the trio approaching, she had a feeling her mood was *not* about to be lifted.

She was right.

"Guess what?" Jessica said, setting her tray down with a bang and looking radiant. "You tell them, Amy," she instructed.

"We've been nominated for All-State!" Amy crowed.

"All-State?" Elizabeth repeated.

"In cheerleading," Jessica explained, giving Amy a triumphant little hug. "We just found out," she explained, sitting down beside Enid and reaching past her for the ketchup to pour on her french fries. "Isn't it incredible? We're going to have a chance to be the best in the whole state!"

"That's great," Enid said automatically.

20

Elizabeth didn't say anything for a minute. "It's fantastic," she said at last, wishing she could make herself feel more excited for her sister and Amy.

And it really *was* fantastic, she told herself sternly. Since when had she ever felt anything but pure delight when something great happened to her twin?

She had never been jealous of Jessica. And she wasn't going to start feeling bad now, just because things seemed to be going so well for her twin. She would never let herself be so unfair. So she tried as hard as she could to sound enthusiastic.

She told herself that her reason for making an excuse to leave the cafeteria early had absolutely nothing to do with Jessica's latest success.

"Liz!" Mr. Collins said as the bell rang, signaling that the period had ended and English class was over. "Can you stay behind for a minute? I've got some news from the Young Writers' Society."

Elizabeth swallowed. Suddenly her mouth felt dry. She had been wondering when the results of the essay contest would be

21

announced, but she'd assumed that the society would contact her by letter. It had never occurred to her that they would notify her faculty sponsor instead.

After the last student had filed out of the classroom, Mr. Collins unfolded a letter that had been lying on his desk. "I think you'll be pleased, Liz," he said, his blue eyes twinkling. "They've awarded you an honorable mention! 'Elizabeth Wakefield has a fresh, natural style, unusual for a girl her age,' he read from the letter. 'We enjoyed her essay very much and will be announcing her name with commendation in our next issue of *Young Writers*.'"

Elizabeth gulped. "Honorable mention. That comes after third place, right?" she asked weakly.

Mr. Collins nodded. "Not bad at all, considering that more than two hundred students entered the contest," he told her. "You're not disappointed, are you?"

Elizabeth shook her head hastily. "Of course not," she said. "To tell you the truth, I wasn't all that happy with the essay I submitted."

"And you're still only a junior," Mr. Collins

reminded her, smiling gently. "There's always next year to clean up with first place."

Elizabeth nodded, barely hearing his words. "Honorable mention," she repeated to herself. She supposed it was better than losing outright.

But it still wasn't winning. And next to Jessica's chance for All-State in cheerleading, it seemed about as mediocre as she could get!

Three

"This chicken is great," Mr. Wakefield said with satisfaction, his dark eyes twinkling as he smiled at his wife. "Alice, you ought to get a superwoman award. I thought you were seeing Nina Davison this afternoon."

Mrs. Wakefield laughed. She had been anxious about meeting Ms. Davison, a VIP from an architecture firm in San Diego. Her full-time business as an interior designer kept Alice Wakefield busy, yet she always looked fresh and well rested when she got home. With her smooth blond pageboy and sky-blue eyes, she didn't look a day over thirty—

certainly not old enough to have a son who was a freshman in college.

"I'm afraid I can't take any credit for dinner tonight, Ned," Mrs. Wakefield told him. "Which one of you was on dinner patrol tonight?" she asked the twins.

"Me," Jessica said blithely, tossing back her golden hair. Elizabeth stared, waiting for her twin to add that all she had done was to reheat a dish Elizabeth had put in the freezer the weekend before. But Jessica was apparently in no mood to admit any such thing.

"Well, this is delicious," her father repeated, grinning at her. Elizabeth gave Jessica the dirtiest look she could, but Jessica was oblivious. It figured, Elizabeth thought moodily. Lately they had been trying to stick more closely to their usual roster. In order to help Mrs. Wakefield, they were alternating nights on kitchen patrol. Whoever was "on" was supposed to prepare the food, set the table, and do the dishes. That way each one could have alternate nights completely free of chores. The only catch was that Jessica still wasn't doing her share. Jessica had a tendency to "forget" all about dinner on the nights she was in charge—or else, she had cheerleading practice, which kept her from getting home early enough to start dinner. And that night, when all she had done was to reheat a meal Elizabeth had prepared, Jessica was praised as though she were Julia Child!

"Anything new at work today?" Mrs. Wakefield asked, helping herself to more salad and smiling at her husband.

But Jessica was too impatient to listen to her father's day. "You're never going to believe in a million years what happened," she burst out.

"Try us," Mr. Wakefield said.

"The cheerleaders got nominated for All-State!" Jessica shrieked, practically leaping out of her chair with excitement. "We didn't think we had a chance. We thought Bayberry Hills Academy would get the nomination instead of us. Can you believe we really have a shot at being the best in the whole *state*?"

"Jess, that's wonderful!" Mrs. Wakefield exclaimed.

"I'm sure it's partly because of Amy joining the team. She's amazingly good," Jessica said, taking a bite of chicken.

"I don't suppose the co-captain had anything to do with it?" Mr. Wakefield said teasingly.

Jessica smiled. "Well . . . maybe just a *lit-*

26

tle," she conceded. "I have to admit that the cheer I invented—you know, the one with the three high kicks and the somersault at the end—probably earned us a bunch of extra points."

"Honey, I think it's terrific. I'm so proud of you," Mrs. Wakefield said, leaning across the table to give her a quick pat.

Elizabeth was staring down at her plate, her face pink. She knew she should say something to Jessica about how great it was, but her heart wasn't in it. Jessica had *everything*. And all *she* had was a crummy honorable mention.

"What about you, Liz? How was your day?" Mr. Wakefield asked.

Elizabeth cleared her throat. "OK," she said at last. "Just an average day."

Mrs. Wakefield looked concerned. "Do you feel all right, sweetheart? You look pale."

"You really do," Jessica seconded. "You should sit out by the pool with me tomorrow afternoon, Liz. We really have to be tan so we'll look great on the slopes at Winter Carnival."

Elizabeth didn't respond to her twin. "I feel fine," she assured her mother. "I guess I'm a little down, that's all. I lost the essay contest I entered," she blurted out. "Mr. Collins got the results today."

"Oh, Liz," Mrs. Wakefield said sadly, putting her hand on her arm. "You must really be disappointed. I know how badly you wanted to win."

Mr. Wakefield cleared his throat. "Well, you gave it your best shot," he told her. "You're really an excellent writer. And if that committee didn't recognize your talents this time, then next year—"

"You sound like Mr. Collins," Elizabeth interrupted glumly. "He thinks an honorable mention isn't that bad and that when I'm a senior I may have a crack at the real prize."

"You got an honorable mention? But that isn't *losing*," Mrs. Wakefield broke in. "Liz, that's *great* news!"

Elizabeth shook her head. "An honorable mention is about as bad as you can do," she pointed out. "It's worse than third place!"

"But, Liz, it's better than all the people who entered and didn't place at all," her mother argued. "Ned, what are we going to do with her?" she demanded, throwing up her hands.

"Your mother's right, Liz," Mr. Wakefield said. "You can't be so hard on yourself, honey. I can understand being disappointed

28

about not winning first prize, but you still have to recognize an honor when you get one!" He sat back and looked at his daughters. "What a talented pair you are," he said, smiling broadly. "I'm proud of you both!"

Elizabeth stared down at her plate. She didn't care what they said. *She* knew an honorable mention wasn't the same as winning. And she could tell from the expression on her sister's face that Jessica secretly agreed.

"It's only an essay contest, anyway," Jessica pointed out. "Come on, Liz. Don't be depressed. Who cares about *essays*?"

Elizabeth tried to stay composed, but she was about to burst into tears. She knew Jessica was trying to make her feel better, but it wasn't working.

"Jess, that isn't very nice," Mrs. Wakefield said reprovingly. "How would you feel if your sister said that about cheerleading?"

Jessica blinked. "Cheerleading," she said, "is different."

"Anything else new?" Mr. Wakefield asked cheerfully, obviously trying to change the subject. Unfortunately Elizabeth's spirits were hardly improved by the next topic Jessica seized upon.

"Amy and I went over to KSVC after school

today to meet Scott Hamlin, the guy who's running the trivia show. It's going to be so much fun," she gushed. "And we also met the competition, two guys from Westwood High. Liz, you should see David Campbell. He's a senior, and he's got the most gorgeous brown eyes that get little wrinkles next to them when he smiles—sort of like yours, Daddy," she added, turning to her father.

"Thanks a lot," Mr. Wakefield said dryly. "That's what I always really wanted to be noticed for—my wrinkles."

"I'm absolutely in love with him," Jessica declared. "I think he's so cute. In fact, I don't see how I'm really going to able to compete with him. He's so smart, too. He knows more trivia than anyone I've ever met."

"Sounds like the beginning of a beautiful friendship," Elizabeth mumbled. She couldn't get worked up about Jessica's latest crush. Not that night.

"You're all going to get to meet him, too. We're going to a movie tonight," Jessica added. "Hey, what time is it?" she demanded, her eyes narrowed.

"It's seven o'clock," said Mrs. Wakefield.

Jessica jumped to her feet, panic-stricken.

"I've got to get ready. He's going to be here in fifteen minutes!"

"Jess," Elizabeth said. "Aren't you forgetting something?"

Jessica stared at her.

"The dishes," Elizabeth pointed out. "It's your night, Jess."

Jessica's eyes widened, and a familiar expression crossed her face. *Ple-e-ease*, Lizzie," she pleaded, wringing her hands and pretending to beg. "Just tonight— I promise I'll do them the next three nights in a row. I *promise*," she added, seeing the incredulous look on her twin's face.

Elizabeth could feel her parents waiting for her response, and she knew they expected her, as always, to be generous and help out her twin. "OK," she mumbled. "But you really—"

Elizabeth never got a chance to finish her warning. Jessica flung herself at her, hugging and kissing her as if Elizabeth had just assured her of winning All-State.

"Go on, you're going to be late for the trivia prince," Elizabeth told her wryly, extricating herself from Jessica's embrace. Her sister flew from the room.

It wasn't that doing the dishes that night

31

was such a big deal. It was the principle that bothered Elizabeth. But she knew there was no point in saying anything to her parents. They were smiling as they watched Jessica's dramatic exit. They obviously thought she was funny. And usually Elizabeth did, too.

It was just that she was beginning to feel that she was being used. It didn't seem fair to her. Elizabeth knew that if something came up on a night when she was supposed to do the dishes, Jessica would never forgive her if she tried to back out of her chores.

As Liz cleared the table, she brooded about her essay. *The truth is that I should've written my essay on a different subject*, she thought. *Instead of calling it "Double or Nothing," I should have called it "Double Standard"!*

Elizabeth knew she was overreacting to what had just transpired, but she also knew that it wasn't the first time it had happened. And if experience was any indicator, it wasn't going to be the last time either.

Jessica was able to get her own way because she charmed people. Elizabeth had been covering up for her for so long that it was almost second nature to her to protect her twin. For example, she would never have told her parents she had prepared that night's dinner. Or that Jessica had been backing out of household chores all too often lately.

The truth was that Elizabeth felt obliged to stick up for Jessica. She knew Jessica counted on her, and Elizabeth wouldn't dream of letting her twin down.

At the same time Elizabeth was beginning to resent Jessica's attitude. And the more she thought about it, the more convinced she became that some things were going to have to be done differently from now on. Otherwise she didn't know what she was going to do.

Four

Elizabeth was proofreading the "Eyes and Ears" column she had just finished typing when the door to *The Oracle* office burst open.

"Hey, I was hoping I'd find you here," Jeffrey said, giving her a big smile.

Elizabeth looked up at him and smiled back. She couldn't help thinking how incredibly handsome he was. His blond hair was glinting a little just then under the lights overhead, and his green eyes twinkled warmly at her. She loved the way he dressed, too—casually preppy—old faded khaki pants and soft pastel sweaters that looked comfortable and sturdy at the same time. Elizabeth was glad the office was deserted, for she knew her expression was giving away what she was feeling.

Jeffrey leaned over her, pretending to scrutinize the page before her. "Hey, you smell nice," he murmured, his nose against her cheek.

Elizabeth shivered as she felt the warmth of his breath. "It's just good old-fashioned soap," she admitted with a giggle. "I wish I could pretend it was something more glamorous, but Jessica borrowed the perfume my father gave me for Christmas, and it seems to be permanently lost somewhere in her room."

"I'll take good old-fashioned soap any day, if it smells this good," Jeffrey said huskily.

Elizabeth cleared her throat, twisting slightly so she could smile up into his green eyes. "You'd better watch it," she said softly. "If you keep talking this way, you might make me forget what I'm doing."

"Now you're catching on!" Jeffrey laughed. "Don't you realize it's a gorgeous day outside? And I didn't come into this office in my capacity as photographer."

"You didn't, huh?" Elizabeth said teasingly. "So what *did* you come in here for, then?"

"In my capacity as a one-man rescue squad. I'm here to save you from yourself, Elizabeth

35

Wakefield," Jeffrey said dramatically. Pulling a chair over, he turned it backward next to her own chair and sat down, facing her, his arms hooked over the rungs. "I happen to have noticed that you've been working too hard these days," he told her, running his fingers lightly up and down her hand. "And there's nothing that gets to me more than watching the love of my life suffering through the doldrums. So guess what I'm going to do for you today?"

"What?" Elizabeth asked with mock seriousness.

"I," Jeffrey said dramatically, "have made reservations for two at what I happen to know is your favorite Italian restaurant. I'm going to drag you out of this office, whisk you away in my chariot—"

"You mean your car?"

"My chariot," Jeffrey corrected her, smiling. "And I'm going to take you home, where you have strict instructions to languish in a bubble bath and keep that wonderful soapy smell of yours. But you have to be ready by six o'clock, or I'm going to turn into a pumpkin. OK?"

Elizabeth shook her head, her blond hair tumbling around her shoulders. "You're too much, Jeffrey French," she said affectionately.

36

"But I have to admit it doesn't sound bad." She cocked her head to one side. "Who knows? I might even find the evening enjoyable."

"I can't tell you how flattered I am," Jeffrey said wryly. He jumped to his feet, his face solemn, and proceeded to bow with utmost seriousness. "Madame, your chariot awaits you," he said, with a wave toward the door.

Elizabeth couldn't suppress her laughter anymore. She had to admit Jeffrey's plan sounded a whole lot better than sitting inside, proofreading.

He was right. It was a beautiful day, and it was going to be a gorgeous evening. The way things had been going lately, she deserved to take some time off to have fun.

Elizabeth felt lucky to have Jeffrey around to cheer her up. As she took his arm she thought his little plan was working. She was feeling a million times better already. And she could hardly wait to sit across from him in a dim, romantic booth at Tiberino's!

"Jess?" Elizabeth called as she opened the front door. There was no answer. Jessica was probably out at the pool, Elizabeth thought, making sure her tan didn't disappear.

Elizabeth hummed as she hung her jacket up in the front hallway. She couldn't believe how much better she felt. She had been making a big fuss over nothing for the past week or so! OK, so Jessica had been a little thoughtless once or twice. That was no big deal. After all, it was probably as much Elizabeth's fault as Jessica's. If Elizabeth had been a little firmer in the past, Jessica would never have gotten accustomed to getting away with shirking chores. And anyway, what was so criminal about leaving the dishes when she had a date? Elizabeth felt herself blush as she recalled how irritated she had been. She vowed to apologize to her twin at the first opportunity.

"Jessica!" she called again, heading through the living room to the glass doors opening out onto the Wakefields' patio. Late-afternoon sunlight streamed across the backyard and the swimming pool, but Jessica was nowhere in sight.

"That's funny," Elizabeth said out loud, her brow furrowing a little. She knew Jessica didn't have cheerleading that day. And it was Jessica's turn to do dinner. She knew Jessica hadn't forgotten, because the twins had talked

38

about it on the way to school that morning. Jessica was planning to make a big salad. "I've decided Daddy needs to watch his weight," she had confided. Elizabeth had burst out laughing at that. Mr. Wakefield was in excellent shape, and in fact, he could still beat Steven at tennis. But Jessica had been adamant. She'd been reading about the dangers of high-cholesterol levels in middle-aged men, and she was determined that the Wakefields should start eating salads at least two nights a week.

Puzzled, Elizabeth strolled back inside, looking for signs of her sister. The house felt ominously quiet. "Aha!" Elizabeth exclaimed, spying a note tucked under a white canister on the kitchen table. She snatched it up and began to read, her eyes darkening as she understood what had happened.

Dear Lizzie—Promise not to be mad at me, but Amy and I need to practice our trivia if we're going to stand a chance next Tuesday. I'm over at the Suttons' and probably won't have time to make the salad. I *swear* I'll make dinner every night for the rest of the week if you just do it for me tonight. Don't be mad! Love, J.

Her hand trembling, Elizabeth put the note down. "Don't be mad," she muttered angrily. Who was Jessica kidding? Of course she was mad! No. That was an understatement. She was *furious*.

There was only one thing Jessica was right about. There was no point in getting angry. Elizabeth took a deep breath, trying to compose herself before storming over to the telephone and dialing the Suttons' phone number. There was no way she was going to let her sister ruin her plans with Jeffrey. As she listened to the phone ring, Elizabeth kept telling herself to stay calm. All she had to do was explain to Jessica that she and Jeffrey had made plans. Jessica would understand at once, apologize, and come home right away and make dinner, the way she was supposed to do from the beginning. And Elizabeth could go to Tiberino's with Jeffrey.

At last the Suttons' housekeeper answered. "Lana? It's Elizabeth Wakefield," Elizabeth said. "I'd like to talk to my sister."

"Oh, dear, you just missed them," Lana said apologetically. "Amy and Jessica went out."

Elizabeth turned pale. "Went out? Where?"

she demanded, twisting the telephone cord anxiously between her fingers.

"I'm not really sure, but I think they may have gone to the library to get some books. Something about finding out what the longest river in Africa is. Does that make sense?"

Elizabeth felt as if she were choking. "Did they say when they were coming back?" she managed.

"No, sweetie, they didn't say," Lana said cheerfully. "You want to leave a message for your sister?"

"Yes," Elizabeth said, trying hard to stay calm. "Tell her to call me *the minute she gets in*. OK?"

"OK," Lana said.

Elizabeth hung up, her eyes stinging with tears. *Now* what was she supposed to do? There was no telling what time Jessica was going to get back. If she went ahead and got ready to go out with Jeffrey, her parents were going to come home tired and hungry, and no dinner would be ready for them. Elizabeth knew she couldn't do that. And if she called her mother, she'd give Jessica away. She was just going to have to call Jeffrey and explain what had happened . . . that she was going to have to take over for Jessica again, and Tiberino's would have to wait.

Jeffrey was disappointed. "You're sure you can't track her down somewhere?" he asked. "It just doesn't seem fair, Liz."

"That's because it isn't," Elizabeth told him. "Look, I'm going to have to have a talk with Jessica when she gets back tonight. But in the meantime I can't let my parents down."

Jeffrey didn't sound convinced. "I think you should just leave it up to Jessica. You and I can go out, and when your parents come home and find out dinner isn't ready, they'll light into her. And you'll be off the hook."

Elizabeth could feel her voice getting higher. "I can't *do* that," she wailed. "Mom's going to be exhausted when she gets back. She's got this rush project, and she's been working really long hours. And Daddy— No, I've got to stick around, Jeffrey. I'm sorry, but we'll just have to do Tiberino's another night."

Jeffrey sighed. "All right, but I think you're making a mistake, Liz," he said finally. "I really think you've got to lay it on the line with Jessica. She's taking advantage of you, and until you make it clear that you're not willing to put up with it, she's not going to stop."

Elizabeth felt her face turn red. "I *said* I was going to talk to her," she said shortly. She couldn't help wishing Jeffrey wouldn't criticize her sister. It was one thing for Elizabeth to complain to him about Jessica, but she instinctively defended her twin whenever anyone else said anything harsh about her. Even when that "anyone else" was Jeffrey.

"Well, I guess that's that," Jeffrey said unhappily. "I'll see you tomorrow in school, then."

Elizabeth didn't respond. She wanted to tell him how terrible she felt about having to cancel their plans, and to tell him again how sweet and crazy he'd been that afternoon—and how much better he'd made her feel. But somehow the whole mood was ruined now. Instead she just ended up muttering something about being sorry, and hung up feeling terrible.

"Hi, honey," Mrs. Wakefield called, coming in through the back door with her arms filled with packages. "Where's Jess?" she added, setting the bags down on one of the kitchen chairs and brushing her hair back with one hand. "Is your father home yet? I ran into tons of traffic downtown. I thought I'd be stuck behind a furniture van all night!"

"Jess is out with Amy Sutton," Elizabeth said shortly, giving her mother a kiss on the cheek. "But Daddy's home. He's upstairs washing his face."

"Jess is with Amy?" Mrs. Wakefield repeated as she slipped out of her jacket. "Oh, well, I'll show *you* what I found for her. It turned out I had about forty-five minutes free this morning, and I had seen a big ad in the paper for The Ski Shop's midwinter sale, so I thought I'd just run in and see"—she was rustling through the bags now—"if I couldn't find something for either of you for Winter Carnival, and sure enough—" She pulled something silver out of the bag and held it up for Elizabeth's inspection. "What do you think? Isn't it perfect for Jessica?"

Elizabeth looked admiringly at the ski suit. "It's wonderful," she breathed, touching the fabric with her forefinger. "What makes it so spangly?"

"It's Lycra, I think. Isn't it super?"

Elizabeth thought it was fantastic. The silver material glowed, and she could tell from the stretchy feel of the cloth that it would fit like a

44

glove. "Jess will look great in it," she said loyally.

Mrs. Wakefield frowned. "I wanted to get *you* something, too, but they really didn't have anything. And I knew you wouldn't go for something like this," she added, looking anxiously at Elizabeth. "Did I do the right thing?"

Elizabeth swallowed. "Of course you did!" she said bravely. "You're right. I'm not really the silver ski suit type. It's much better for Jessica."

"Good," Mrs. Wakefield said, looking immensely relieved. "I'm sure you and I will find something. Maybe we can look this weekend."

"I don't really need a new ski suit," Elizabeth said, fingering the lovely silver material again. "But you're sweet to have thought of it, anyway."

"Well, we'll see—maybe this weekend . . ." Mrs. Wakefield murmured, putting the silver ski suit back into the bag. "I'm going to say hello to your father and change my clothes," she said, hurrying out of the kitchen. Elizabeth was left alone, a forlorn look on her face.

She knew it was childish, but she couldn't help wishing her mother had bought the ski suit for her instead of Jessica. It wasn't really her sort of thing, but for once, just for once, she wished she weren't pigeonholed as the conservative twin, the one who'd be happier in navy down than silver Lycra.

It just seemed a lot more fun to be Jessica than Elizabeth these days. And she felt as though she had to do something about it—and fast!

Five

"Hi, everybody!" Jessica called from the front hallway. "Sorry I'm late. Amy and I were at the library trying to find out what the longest river in Africa is." Jessica shrugged out of her jacket, her cheeks flushed as she giggled, remembering. "Only we ended up getting sidetracked. Do you know that the record for most marriages in a single lifetime is held by a woman from Toledo, Ohio?"

"Jess, we started dinner without you," Mrs. Wakefield said reproachfully as Jessica entered the dining room. "We had no idea when you were planning on coming back. Why didn't you call?"

Jessica sat down at her place. "I had no idea we'd be so long," she said apologetically. She turned to Elizabeth, her eyes pleading. "You're not mad at me about dinner, are you, Liz? I promise I'll do it every night for the rest of the week."

Elizabeth didn't answer. She was staring at the mulberry sweater her sister was wearing. "Isn't that my sweater?" she asked.

Jessica stared down at what she was wearing. "Oh . . . yeah, I guess it is," she admitted, a look of confusion crossing her face. "I would've asked you if I could borrow it, but you weren't home, and I just sort of . . ." Her voice trailed off.

"You just sort of took it without asking," Elizabeth supplied. "Right?" Since her own taste was conservative, it amazed Elizabeth that Jessica borrowed so many of her things. But, then, Elizabeth thought, Jessica always liked to appear in new clothes.

Mrs. Wakefield cleared her throat. "Girls, I think we should save this sort of discussion for someplace other than the dinner table. Jessica, would you like some salad?"

Jessica nodded and quickly helped herself. Then she eyed her sister nervously. "I really didn't think you'd mind," she hissed conspiratorially.

Elizabeth could feel an angry flush creeping up her neck and face. "You know that sweater was a present from Enid," she said hotly. "I've only worn it twice."

"Liz," Mr. Wakefield said repovingly, "you heard your mother. Conversation at the dinner table should be pleasant and edifying, which means no squabbling over sweaters!"

Elizabeth dropped her eyes guiltily. She knew her parents must think she was acting like a two-year-old. In fact, from the expression of concern on Mrs. Wakefield's face Elizabeth guessed that her mother was wondering why she was being so stingy. It wasn't like Elizabeth to object to something as trivial as a borrowed sweater.

But that was part of the problem, she realized now. Jessica just felt that she could walk all over her! In fact, she couldn't remember the last time she had said no to her sister about *anything*. No wonder Jessica was taking advantage of her now!

"I have a feeling this trivia hunt you and Amy are involved in may prove to be a good thing," Mr. Wakefield was saying, obviously trying to change the subject as he turned to

Jessica. "You girls may actually learn quite a bit."

Jessica grimaced. "We're not *learning*, Daddy," she corrected him. "We're just having a good time." She frowned, taking a bite of salad. "The problem is that David and his partner, Jake, are really going to be fierce competition. I was sort of hoping David would offer to let us win, especially since he asked me out again and everything. But he seems like he's the competitive type."

"I'm sure it's better anyway," Mrs. Wakefield said, taking a sip of iced tea. "You wouldn't want to win just because the competition wasn't trying, would you?"

"Well, if we win, we get to be the first contestants on the new game show they're starting," Jessica told her. "So we want to win, no matter what!"

"Well, we'll just all have to start testing you." Mr. Wakefield laughed. "For instance, how many states can you think of that begin with *M*?"

Jessica stared blankly at him. "Uh—Maine," she muttered, reaching for a roll. "Missouri. Michigan. Montana. I think that's all."

"Massachusetts, Mississippi, and Maryland," Mr. Wakefield reminded her with a smile.

"You forgot Minnesota," Mrs. Wakefield said, laughing.

"They're not going to ask us things like that, are they?" Jessica wailed, looking panicky.

Elizabeth sat quietly, thinking that she had a list of questions of her own for her twin. Like where she got her nerve—and how she thought she could get away with the things she got away with.

But she had a feeling she had better wait until they were upstairs to start the quiz.

"I'll do the dishes!" Jessica said generously, jumping up from the table and beginning to clear it. She had obviously forgotten it was her turn to do them anyway. From the look she was giving her twin, it was clear she thought she was being incredibly noble!

Jessica was grimacing at herself in the mirror when Elizabeth knocked at her bedroom door. "Come in!" she yelled, pinching her cheeks to see if her muscle tone was improving.

"What's wrong with you?" Elizabeth demanded, coming into her sister's bedroom

51

with a frown. "You look as though you swallowed poison or something."

"Lila told me that if you do facial exercises every night you'll never get wrinkles," Jessica explained. "We were talking about Ms. Dalton, and Lila thinks she must do them because she hardly has any wrinkles." Lila Fowler was one of Jessica's closest friends. She was also from one of the wealthiest families in Sweet Valley and seemed to be a constant crusade to enhance her beauty. She spent a small fortune on makeovers, exercise classes, and trips to spas.

"Ms. Dalton's only twenty-five or twenty-six," Elizabeth pointed out. "Don't you think that might have something to do with it?"

Jessica stared at her sister, her blue-green eyes round. Elizabeth sure sounded crabby lately, she thought. "We didn't mean it as an *insult*," she protested, enunciating her vowels as much as possible to help stretch her cheek muscles. "Liz, aren't you dying for it to be next weekend already? I can't *wait* for Winter Carnival. Just think, Steve'll be there," she added jubilantly, sure the mention of their older brother would lift her sister's spirits.

But Elizabeth was still glowering at her.

"What is it?" Jessica asked uneasily.

"You're not still mad about your sweater, are you? I honestly had no idea you'd be so upset. I mean, I know I shouldn't have taken it, but I couldn't find a single mulberry thing anywhere, and I promised Amy I'd wear these new pants. She wanted to see them on me, and I didn't have anything to go with them, and I thought—"

"I'm not just angry about the sweater," Elizabeth interrupted her, "though I do think it was wrong of you not to wait. Wouldn't you be furious if I came rummaging through your closet and just took whatever I felt like?"

Jessica looked thoughtfully into her closet, which looked, even on its best days, more like a laundry hamper than anything else. Jessica's room was a subject of long-standing friction in the Wakefield household, which was generally very neat. "How you ever find your way from your bed to your dresser is beyond me," Mrs. Wakefield had said once when she had risked opening the door and looking inside. Jessica usually took criticism well, since she was convinced her own methods were best. When it came to her closet, she was particularly resistant to criticism. "You're welcome to anything you want," she told Elizabeth now, entirely genuine in her generosity. "Liz, you know I don't care if you borrow things." She frowned, surveying her twin's cords and crew-neck sweater. "I just don't know if you'd really *want* anything of mine. But you know you're welcome to look."

Elizabeth's eyes darkened. "You know that isn't the point," she said angrily. "Jess, do you have any idea how many times you've backed out of doing dinner lately?"

Jessica thought quickly. She had been afraid a question like this was coming, and in part she was ready for it. "It can't be more than once or twice," she tried first, avoiding her sister's piercing gaze.

"Three times in two weeks," Elizabeth corrected, folding her arms and scowling at her. "Three times, Jess! That's ridiculous. It isn't fair! It means I've had to break the plans I've made so often that from now on I'm going to be afraid to make plans at all, because I won't know whether or not I can count on you to be around to get dinner ready."

Jessica blinked. "You're sure I've really missed *three* times?" She didn't see much point in arguing. Knowing Elizabeth, she probably had been keeping track. And three times did seem kind of bad. "I feel awful," she said.

Elizabeth, her arms still folded, kept glaring at her.

"Did you miss anything tonight?" Jessica asked anxiously.

"Oh, just going out to Tiberino's with Jeffrey. Nothing special," Elizabeth said sarcastically.

Jessica swallowed nervously. It wasn't like her sister to look so upset. And Elizabeth was almost never sarcastic. *She must really be angry!* Jessica thought.

"I feel terrible," Jessica said in a low voice. "Lizzie, please forgive me! I feel like a rat. If I'd known—"

"Jess, that's the whole point!" Elizabeth burst out. "You never know because you don't *think*. You just assume I won't have any plans or that what I'm doing isn't as important as what you're doing. You mean well, but you're not very considerate when it comes to me and my feelings. And I just feel I can't keep quiet about it any longer!"

Jessica felt her eyes filling with tears. If there was one thing in the world she couldn't stand, it was having Elizabeth mad at her. "Please forgive me, Liz," she begged. "I've been such a jerk, but I promise—no, I *swear*—it won't happen again! Trust me, Liz. I swear I'll be more thoughtful. I don't blame you one little bit if you never speak to me again, but I won't be able to stand it, so please—I'm not kidding, Liz, *please* don't hate me!"

Elizabeth laughed. "You make me sound like a monster," she said reproachfully. "Jess, the point isn't my hating you. I just wanted to clear the air. I feel like you and I need to be equally respectful of each other, which goes for not breaking commitments, not borrowing things without asking—the whole works."

"You're right," Jessica said solemnly. "You're absolutely right. Liz, if you don't promise to forgive me right now, I'm going to have a fit!"

"All right," Elizabeth said, relenting. "I forgive you, Jess." She shook her head. "I don't know what it is about you, but you ought to bottle it and put it on sale."

"What do you mean?" Jessica demanded indignantly.

"I mean," Elizabeth said with a laugh, "that it's absolutely impossible to stay angry with you! Not," she added darkly, "that I haven't had plenty of good reasons to lately."

Jessica knew the crisis was past. "You're too hard on me," she said self-pityingly, sniffing a little. "I can't help it if I'm a little thoughtless

56

every once in a while. It's just because *you're* so perfect, Liz. Everyone is always telling me how I should try to act like *you* do. Do you think that's easy to live with?"

Elizabeth rolled her eyes. "Please," she said. "Do you think it's any easier being the one everyone always thinks of as Goody Two Shoes? Like that," she added, pointing to the silver ski suit lying amidst a jumble of other clothes on Jessica's bed. "How would you like it if Mom took one look at that and said it looked perfect for me—and that *you* would naturally look better in something navy-blue and puffy?"

Jessica thought that over. "Do you want to borrow it?" she asked quickly, hoping to make amends. "I think you'd look great in silver, Liz."

Elizabeth sighed. "No," she said finally. "Thanks for offering, Jess—but Mom's right. I *would* look better in navy-blue. Let's face it, Jessica. The die is cast. You're you, and I'm me, and wherever we go people are going to expect me to be on time and to wear navy-blue and they're *not* going to expect you to do either."

Jessica stared at her sister. She couldn't imagine a worse fate than the one Elizabeth was describing for herself. *Poor Liz,* she thought, her turquoise eyes widening as she turned the dilemma over and over again in her mind.

"It's OK." Elizabeth laughed, seeing the horrified expression in her sister's eyes. "It's really not *that* awful, Jess. But do me a favor, OK?"

"Sure," Jessica said, ready to do anything Elizabeth asked right then. "Name it!"

"Just don't make it worse by thinking that way yourself," Elizabeth begged her. " 'Cause every once in a while *I* feel like being a little wild and irresponsible myself. And unless you're around to count on, there's no way I can do it."

"I promise," Jessica said, giving her sister a hug. "Don't worry," she added. "You can count on me, Liz. Honest." She was absolutely certain that no matter what happened in the next few weeks, at least *she* wouldn't give her sister any reason to feel overburdened or angry again!

Six

"Look, you two," Winston Egbert said dramatically, stepping up to the crowded table where Jessica and Amy were firing questions at each other from the *Guinness Book of World Records*. "If you really have any hope of winning on Tuesday afternoon, you're going to need coaching from the king of trivia."

It was Friday at lunchtime, and Jessica and Amy were both in high spirits—especially Jessica, who was looking forward to her date with David Campbell that evening. A crowd had gathered around them, and both girls were enjoying the attention their practice was getting. Until Winston arrived, that is. Jessica did not find the tall, gangly junior half as amusing as some of her classmates seemed to. And just then she thought he was a royal pain.

"Come on, Winston," she scoffed. "What do *you* know about trivia?"

Winston clutched his heart, pretending to swoon with pain. "She's hurt my pride," he cried. Ken Matthews and Bill Chase burst out laughing. "I'm serious," Winston said. "Look, guys, you know what a trivia god I am. *You* tell her what she's done to me, pretending to forget my heroic feats."

"Winston, you're weird," Amy Sutton said, giggling.

"For example," Winston went on, clearing his throat and taking a chair near Jessica and Amy, "what was the name of the ship Charles Darwin sailed on during his most famous voyage?"

Jessica and Amy exchanged stricken glances. "Charles *Darwin*?" Jessica repeated incredulously.

"Something every trivia fiend should know," Winston said reprovingly.

Amy looked upset. "What was it called?" she asked Jessica.

Jessica gave Winston a dirty look. "Ask

something else," she instructed him. "No one's going to ask us about Charles Darwin!"

"OK." Winston scratched his head, thinking hard. "But for you information, it was called the *Beagle*." He thought for a minute. "What are the first two letters on every boat registration in the state of California?"

"They're not going to ask us *that*!" Jessica shrieked.

Amy looked confused. "What if they do?" she demanded. "What are they, Winston?"

"*CF*," Winston said with evident satisfaction. "Girls, you two need a little work," he added, pretending to ignore the scattered applause that broke out around the table when he answered his own question. "I'd be willing to coach you—for a small fee, of course. But we're going to have to get started right away if your big day is Tuesday."

Jessica's eyes darkened. "I'm sure we're going to do just fine," she said loftily. "Don't worry," she added reassuringly, patting Amy's arm. "I promise we're going to do incredibly well." *And even if we don't, after tonight I'm sure I'll be able to convince David to make sure we win*, she thought. Jessica was positive David would throw the contest once he and Jessica had *really* started going out. So far they'd had only two casual dates. But once things got romantic, she was sure he'd be as eager for Jessica and Amy to win as the girls were themselves.

Not that Jessica was interested in David only for that reason—far from it! In fact, Jessica had butterflies in her stomach just thinking about David Campbell. She hadn't been this interested in a guy in a long time.

But it had struck her that if she could make David fall madly in love with her, one dividend would be that David would never allow himself to let her lose. And what could be better than being allowed to win a big trivia show by your brand-new boyfriend?

"Hey, Jessica, come down off your cloud and talk to us earth people," Winston joked, snapping his fingers under her nose.

Jessica started, then gave him a dirty look. But she knew Winston was right. This wasn't the time or place to daydream about David Campbell. That, she thought, smiling, would have to wait until later.

Elizabeth hummed to herself as she climbed the stairs to her bedroom. Friday afternoon— just a week until Winter Carnival! It was incredible how quickly her spirits had been lifted, which made her realize that it really was Jessica who had been upsetting her. Now that they had talked, Elizabeth was feeling much more like her old self. She couldn't believe she had been so critical of Jessica. After all, what had Jessica really done wrong—borrow a sweater without asking? Shirk dinner duty a few times?

Elizabeth smiled as she threw her books down on the chair in the corner of her bedroom. It was Friday, and she was in good mood, with the whole weekend to look forward to. And she was inclined to forgive her sister for everything, now that they were back on their usual good terms.

Elizabeth glanced at her watch, then walked into the bathroom that joined the twins' rooms. She knocked loudly on Jessica's door. "Come in!" her sister yelled over the sound of her stereo, which was turned to top volume. Elizabeth opened the door gingerly, her eyes widening at the sight that greeted her. Jessica was ransacking her dresser, tearing clothes out with terrifying speed, scrutinizing each garment, and then either balling it up and stuffing it back into the dresser or tossing it helter-skelter onto the bed.

"What's happening in here?"

"I'm trying to find something to wear tonight," Jessica muttered. "This is too bright . . . too small . . . too funky," she kept saying feverishly. "Oh, Liz, what am I going to do?" she cried at last, stricken. "I want to look really great tonight!"

Elizabeth regarded the pile of clothes on the bed. "If you can't find something in that mountain of stuff, I don't know where else you'll find anything."

"See, I want to have just the right look," Jessica confided, shaking out a wrinkled silk tunic. "Where did *this* come from?" she mumbled, more to herself than to her sister. "David's very particular about the way women dress, I think. His mother owns a boutique in the mall—you know that little one with the really expensive clothes we never go into? It's called Bibi's?"

"Oh, yeah. The one with all those strange mannequins in the window."

Jessica nodded. "I think she's really high-fashion. And David's sister Barbara is meeting us somewhere tonight with Mitch, her boyfriend, and David makes her sound like the most glamorous thing ever." She threw the tunic down. "I don't have a thing to wear," she declared miserably.

Elizabeth laughed. "Well, you're welcome to anything of mine," she said generously. "I won't be needing anything special to wear tonight. In fact, that's what I came in here for, Jess. I need to ask you a big favor."

"Sure," Jessica murmured, turning back to her dresser drawer.

"I'm supposed to baby-sit for Teddy Collins tonight," Elizabeth said, sitting gingerly on the edge of Jessica's bed in an effort not to crumple any of the clothes strewn all over it. Teddy was Mr. Collins's six-year-old son. After his divorce, Mr. Collins had won custody of the adorable little boy. "Actually, I'm not really baby-sitting," she corrected herself, watching Jessica's whirlwind activity with amusement. "Mr. Collins is away for the weekend, so Heather's staying over both nights." Heather was Mr. Collins's sister, who lived nearby and had agreed to stay with Teddy.

Jessica looked as if she wasn't following very closely. "Uhm-hmm," she murmured, seizing a black oversize vest and examining it closely.

"But Heather doesn't drive," Elizabeth

65

pointed out. "That's where I come in. Apparently Teddy's gone to a birthday party at Ricky Alden's, and he needs a ride home. I'm supposed to pick him up when the party's over and take him back to Mr. Collins's."

Jessica made a little noise, apparently meant to show she was still listening. "Liz, what do you think of this?" she demanded, holding the vest up in front of her.

"It's nice," Elizabeth said. "Jess, are you listening to any of this? I need to ask you a big favor." She checked her watch again. "Mr. Alden is going to call sometime after six to let me know what time to pick Teddy up and to leave directions to his house. But I promised Jeffrey I'd play tennis with him this afternoon, and I don't think I'll be back before six-thirty. And Mom and Dad are going out to dinner straight from work. Could you just take the message for me and let Mr. Alden know I'll definitely be there to get Teddy?"

"Sure," Jessica said, putting on a bright-pink long-sleeved shirt. "Where are you guys playing tennis?"

"The grass courts at the park," Elizabeth said, jumping up off the bed. "So you promise you'll get all that down? The time I should get him and the directions?"

"I promise." Jessica laughed. "Don't be such a worrywart," she added. "David isn't picking me up until seven. I *promise*," she added, giggling at the concerned look on her sister's face. She slipped the vest over her shirt.

Elizabeth looked at her dubiously. "I don't know about that vest, Jess. Don't you think it's kind of . . . I don't know, kind of *big*?"

Jessica inspected herself in the full-length mirror on the back of the bedroom door. "Big is in," she replied, pivoting a little in front of the glass. The vest hung down loosely over the tight black stirrup pants Jessica was wearing. "This is perfect," Jessica declared admiringly. "Even David's sister won't be able to object."

Elizabeth laughed. "Well, whatever you decide to wear, don't forget the message," she repeated, stepping out into the hall.

Jessica gave her a doleful look. "You don't trust me," she said mournfully. "You don't even think I can handle a simple set of directions."

Elizabeth felt herself relenting. "All right, all right," she said. She didn't have time to stick around berating her sister, anyway. She had to meet Jeffrey in less than half an hour, and she couldn't even remember where she'd left her tennis racket.

Besides, even Jessica could handle this, she assured herself. What on earth could possibly go wrong?

"Perfect," Jessica declared, studying herself in the mirror. It had taken ages, but she was finally convinced she looked good—even good enough for David Campbell. Now all she had to do was wait for seven to roll around.

To her surprise, she heard a car pull into the drive. It was only six-fifteen. Maybe it was Elizabeth coming back early, Jessica thought. She gave her hair a few furious last-minute strokes with her brush and was just applying her lip gloss when the door bell rang. It *couldn't* be Elizabeth then. Jessica frowned, peering out the window down at the drive below. It was David's blue MG! *What's he doing here this early?* she asked herself. She grabbed frantically at her purse and instantly decided she hated what she was wearing.

"I'm sorry I'm so early," David said apologetically when she opened the front door a few moments later. He took his sunglasses off and smiled at her. "Barbara and Mitch called a little while ago, and they want us to meet them at seven at a Japanese restaurant that's about half an hour away. So I thought we'd better get an early start."

Jessica was so busy thinking how wonderful David looked that she barely noticed what he'd said—or registered the fact that they were going out for Japanese food, which she had never tried—and had never *wanted* to try very much, either. David looked great. He was wearing loose, well-worn chinos that were faded just the right amount. He had a great tan, and he was making the most of it with a pale yellow shirt and a white sweater that was knotted around his neck. He had just the sort of looks Jessica loved—dark, handsome, and ultracool.

"Uh-oh," Jessica said suddenly, hearing the telephone ring. "Hang on a second, David. I have to grab the phone." The next minute she was listening to Mr. Alden explain that the birthday party would be breaking up around six-thirty. Jessica explained that her sister wouldn't be coming home until then but that she'd leave her a message with the time and the directions. "Don't worry about Teddy," she told him, impressed with her own efficiency. "Liz'll be there as soon as she can."

Jessica took down the directions he gave her on a slip of paper from her father's desk, and after she had hung up, she checked them twice to make sure they were legible. *What a good sister I am,* she thought with a little smile. There was no way she was going to let Elizabeth down again!

"Jess, we should probably get going if we're going to make it by seven," David called from the front hall.

Suddenly Jessica had a million things to do. She had to lock both doors, find her makeup kit, turn off all the lights, comb her hair again, and run back upstairs to get some money. In all the excitement she had absolutely no idea that she had taken the note for Elizabeth and slipped it in her purse.

"Got everything?" David asked, smiling down at her as he opened the front door.

"Yep!" Jessica exclaimed. As she followed him out to his car, she could hardly wait for the evening to get started.

Seven

An hour later Jessica was snuggled next to David in a dimly lit booth in A Taste of Tokyo. Barbara and Mitch were across from them, masterfully eating pieces of sashimi with their chopsticks.

"Why aren't you eating anything, Jessica?" Barbara asked, giving Jessica a slightly critical look.

Jessica swallowed. The thought of raw fish just didn't appeal to her, but she didn't want to be a bad sport. Barbara and Mitch were eating the tiny morsels with evident enjoyment— but then Barbara and Mitch were different. Barbara was nineteen, but she acted as if she were about twenty-nine. She treated David and Jessica like two-year-olds. Mitch was even worse. He kept talking about Hollywood and going into "film," and he was wearing the weirdest clothes—an oversize Hawaiian shirt fastened at the throat with a jeweled pin, and strangely cut linen pants that made him look emaciated. His glasses were kelly green, and when Jessica made a remark about them, Mitch gave her a scornful look. "I have twenty-five pair of glasses," he told her. "I change them to go with what I'm wearing."

Jessica couldn't help wondering about Mitch and Barbara. Fortunately David didn't seem to take after his older sister at all. He was evidently enjoying her company but was focusing most of his energy and attention on Jessica. He seemed proud to be her date, which delighted Jessica. It was worth putting up with a slightly eccentric older sister—and a platter of raw fish—for a chance to get to know David better.

"You really ought to try the sashimi, Jess," Barbara said reprovingly, picking up an ivory-colored piece of raw fish with her chopsticks. "It's delicious."

Jessica picked up her chopsticks and gave Barbara a cooperative smile. She didn't think it was a good idea to antagonize her, in case Barbara had any influence on David. "I'd love to try some," she lied, reaching for the closest piece. It didn't look much like fish, but then none of this stuff looked the way it ought to. It was a green pasty ball, and Jessica had a problem picking it up with her chopsticks. Barbara was too busy feeding a silvery piece of fish to Mitch to notice that Jessica had taken the fiery-hot horseradish by mistake. And David didn't notice till Jessica had already popped it into her mouth.

"Oh, no!" he exclaimed, quickly pouring her a glass of water. "Drink some of this," he commanded, holding it up to her mouth.

Jessica felt as if her mouth were in flames. Sputtering and coughing, her face about as red as the tablecloth, she reached for the glass. It was several minutes before she could thank him. Barbara and Mitch were looking on with a mixture of concern and amusement, which didn't make her feel much better. So much for sashimi, she thought furiously, digging through her bag to find a tissue.

"Oh, *no!*" she gasped, pulling out the note with the directions to Mr. Alden's house scrawled on it. She forgot all about the burning horseradish she had just swallowed. All she could think about was Elizabeth, waiting anxiously for Mr. Alden's call and not knowing what to do.

"Will you excuse me? I have to make a phone call," she said hastily, sliding out of the booth with the note in her hand. She noticed that Barbara was giving her a strange look, but Jessica didn't care.

She couldn't believe she had been so careless. Elizabeth was going to kill her! And after she'd sworn to be more responsible about everything, too.

It took several minutes for Jessica to find the pay phone and get change for a dollar. Then someone else was using the phone, and she had to wait. Finally she dialed the Wakefields' number. The phone rang twelve times before she hung up, frustrated and upset. Where was Elizabeth? Had she managed to get through to Mr. Alden even without the note?

Jessica could see David laughing with his sister and Mitch as she approached the table, and she decided then and there to put Elizabeth out of her mind for the time being. It wasn't as though there was anything she could do about it now anyway. Besides, Jessica knew she'd be able to explain to Elizabeth when she got home. It was an accident, she rationalized. And accidents could happen to anybody.

"I had a really nice time tonight," Jessica said huskily. She and David were parked in front of the Wakefields' house. It was late, and the only light was coming from Elizabeth's room upstairs.

"I had a nice time, too," David said, putting his arm behind her along the car seat. "I'm sorry if my sister was kind of weird. She's a nice girl, but she can act pretty affected at times."

"I thought she was really nice," Jessica lied. She leaned back a little, so that David's arm was touching her shoulders. "I bet you and Jake have really been working hard, reviewing your trivia for Tuesday," she said casually.

David's eyes crinkled up at the corners. "Hey, let's not mix business and pleasure," he said, letting his hand drop to her shoulder and pulling her closer to him.

Jessica glanced quickly at him. That didn't sound quite as promising as she had hoped. "You know, winning the contest on Tuesday would mean an awful lot to my partner, Amy," she said softly, brushing his fingers with her own. "*I* don't really care that much about things like that, but Amy has her heart set on winning. It would just be such a *shame* for her if we didn't win," she added, looking up at David from lowered lashes. She tried to look helpless and sweet, but David didn't seem to be cooperative. In fact, he was grinning at her.

"Tonight is Friday," he said, putting his hands on her shoulders and looking down deep into her eyes. "And as far as I'm concerned, tonight I'd give in to anything you asked, Jessica. But Tuesday is Tuesday. And I'm afraid I'm just no good at trying to lose. So I guess it'll just have to be every person for himself."

Jessica could feel herself pouting a little. "That's not very nice," she said, pulling back from him, a hurt expression in her eyes.

David burst out laughing. "You don't really expect me to let you win on Tuesday, do you?"

Jessica glared at him. She didn't know *what* she expected, but after putting up with his sister and practically killing herself on a lump of horseradish, she thought she deserved more consideration than this. "I have to go in now," she said, opening the car door on her side.

David put his hand on hers. "Wait, Jess, I really had fun tonight. Don't be mad at me."

Jessica pulled away from him. "I've got to go study some more trivia," she told him. "There's no way I'm going to let you win on Tuesday!"

"Good. I like a girl who's competitive." David chuckled. "But I'd better warn you— Jake and I are really hot. We're going to be pretty tough to beat."

Jessica got out of the car. "Thanks for everything," she said angrily, slamming the car door shut and hurrying into the house. She couldn't believe what a jerk he had turned out to be. Any decent guy would have promised not to win—or at least to try not to make the competition too difficult.

But David Campbell obviously wasn't a decent guy. He was a jerk, she told herself, digging in her bag for her house keys. A complete and total jerk.

Still, she couldn't help noticing that he didn't start his car until she was safely inside. A jerk, but a considerate jerk, she thought.

All in all, it looked as though Tuesday was going to be pretty interesting.

*   *   *

"Liz?" Jessica said softly, knocking on her sister's door. She didn't hear anything at first and knocked again.

"Come in," Elizabeth said. She didn't sound friendly, but Jessica was so busy thinking about David that she barely noticed.

"Hey, I'm so sorry about messing up Mr. Alden's message," Jessica said, hurrying in and plopping down on the end of her sister's bed. Elizabeth was reading in bed, but she set her novel down when Jessica came in. Her face was stony.

"I hope I didn't mess everything up," Jessica said, leaning over to examine a small scuff mark on her black flats. "Liz, I'm so glad you're still up. I *have* to tell you what just happened with David."

Elizabeth cleared her throat angrily. "Jessica," she said coldly. "Do you have any idea what an idiot I looked like tonight?"

Jessica regarded her sister. "What do you mean?"

"What I *mean*," Elizabeth said sternly, "is that when I got back from playing tennis, there was no message. Nothing. So I hung around, assuming that Mr. Alden just hadn't called before you left. Finally I decided to go ahead and call him, just to make sure there hadn't been any confusion. And guess what?"

"What?" Jessica repeated, her expression innocent.

"He wasn't there," Elizabeth snapped. "You know where he was?"

"How would I know where he was?" Jessica asked, injured.

"He was driving Teddy back to Mr. Collins's house, because he'd left a message here and I never came! Can you imagine how intelligent I felt when I finally got through to him and found out what had happened?"

Jessica found a piece of gum in her purse and unwrapped it slowly. "Well, it doesn't sound *that* bad," she said at last, popping the gum into her mouth. "I mean, at least Teddy got home safely. It could've been worse."

"Jessica," Elizabeth said angrily, "the point is that I looked totally irresponsible! I promised Mr. Collins that I'd pick Teddy up, and I didn't come through! Instead Mr. Alden had to take him home. And you know whose fault it was that I looked so irresponsible?"

"I guess it was mine," Jessica said, chewing. She thought Elizabeth was making too big a deal out of the whole thing. Mr. Collins was hardly going to care who had driven little

Teddy home from Ricky Alden's birthday party! "Listen, Liz, I'm sorry. I really am. I was just totally flustered, and somehow I threw the message in my purse." She shook her head, remembering. "You wouldn't blame me if you had any idea how traumatic everything was. David was almost an hour early, and—"

"I don't think you understand," Elizabeth interrupted, her eyes blazing. "Jess, the point is that I asked you for a favor, and you *promised*. How could you just accidentally take the message with you? Don't you realize how worried I was? How *stupid* I felt?"

Jessica stared at her twin. "Look, I said I was sorry. I have no idea how I managed to mess up. But I tried calling you, and you weren't home."

"I went over to Mr. Alden's, to apologize."

"Oh, good. Then it's all OK!" Jessica said, brightening. "You can't be mad at me, Liz. I have to ask your advice about David."

"Well, I *am* mad at you," Elizabeth retorted, grabbing her novel and flipping the pages furiously. "And I don't want to hear about David," she added, glaring at Jessica. "I think you need to think about what a promise means, Jessica Wakefield. And I think it's high time you started taking your responsibilities a little more seriously."

Jessica got up and picked up her purse. "Well, I guess I'd better go study some trivia," she said, hoping Elizabeth could be sidetracked onto a new topic of conversation—one that could lead to David and Tuesday.

Elizabeth just ignored her and pretended to read her novel. Jessica was forced to leave without asking her sister's advice about her date.

Jessica frowned as she walked to her bedroom. She couldn't believe Elizabeth was so mad about one silly little message. Something else must be bothering her, Jessica decided. And it was up to her to find out what it was.

Eight

Jessica was lying flat on her back on the diving board of the Wakefields' pool, thinking how wonderful Saturdays were. What a perfect afternoon! She had the whole house to herself, too. Elizabeth had gone off to spend the day with Jeffrey, and both Mr. and Mrs. Wakefield were catching up on work downtown. It was one of those Southern California winter days that might have been the middle of summer, and Jessica was taking advantage of it, basking in the sun so her tan would be perfect for the following weekend. She was thinking about a dozen different things: the likelihood of being asked science questions on Tuesday; whether or not she should get her hair cut before the carnival; why Elizabeth was still being so grumpy and what to do about it; that she was supposed to meet Elizabeth and Jeffrey at the Dairi Burger at five with a bunch of other people.

She squinted up at the sun, making sure she was still in the best position for maximum tanning, then stretched languidly, closed her eyes, and went back to her jumbled thoughts. Too bad David had been so wretched the night before, she thought, or something wonderful might have come of their friendship. He was out in the cold now. There was no way she was going to give him the pleasure of dating her, not after his behavior about the trivia contest!

Suddenly Jessica's eyes flew open. The phone was ringing inside. Grabbing her towel, she hurried across the patio and opened the sliding door, reaching the telephone in the study on the fifth ring.

"Liz?" a familiar voice asked.

Jessica's brow wrinkled. "Todd Wilkins!" she exclaimed. "It isn't Liz. It's Jessica," she added hastily, plopping down on a chair and tucking her legs underneath her. "I haven't heard your voice in *ages*. How are you?" she asked. She couldn't believe her luck. Here she had been hoping for a chance to get to the bottom of Elizabeth's bad mood, and now she had a likely suspect right on the line!

Jessica had her doubts about Elizabeth and Todd's breakup. She knew Todd had supposedly fallen in love with Suzanne Devlin and that Elizabeth insisted their friendship had cooled off due to separation. But Jessica couldn't give up the idea that they were still attached to each other. She had been wondering if Elizabeth's current bad mood might have something to do with Todd's imminent visit. After all, that would make sense. Here Elizabeth had convinced herself that she and Todd were just friends. But now that Todd was planning to come to Sweet Valley for Winter Carnival, it was only natural for her *real* feelings to resurface. Or so Jessica speculated as she listened to Todd telling her how cold it was in Vermont and how much he was looking forward to his visit to Sweet Valley.

"I know Liz is going to be so upset she missed you," Jessica said coyly, twisting the telephone cord around one finger. She didn't see much point in telling the poor boy that her sister was out with Jeffrey. Why make him feel bad? she thought. "Can I give her a message?"

she asked, trying to make her voice inviting enough so that Todd could break down and confess how much he still loved Elizabeth.

All Todd said, though, was that the dinner for Friday night was still on. "I know Liz was planning on going up to the carnival on Friday afternoon, but the PTA awards banquet is that night. Tell Liz I'll completely understand if she can't make the dinner, OK? Just ask her to call me when she gets a chance to let me know."

"I promise I'll tell her," Jessica said, writing the message out with special care. After the previous evening she wasn't going to risk getting another message wrong. "Anything else?" she asked meaningfully.

"No, that's it," Todd replied. "Except that I'm looking forward to seeing you both."

Jessica raised her eyebrows. She was sure he was! It was really kind of heartbreaking. But she knew she shouldn't interfere. She wasn't going to risk meddling—not at this point, with Elizabeth getting angry at the slightest provocation.

No, she was simply going to give her sister the phone message, word for word.

Jessica was going to do everything right from now on. She had too much to worry about without having to be anxious about

Elizabeth's being angry. With a wave of self-righteousness, Jessica folded the piece of paper with the message on it into a neat square and left it on the desk, where she'd be sure to remember it.

She was going to get *this* message to her sister if it killed her!

Elizabeth scooped up a spoonful of vanilla ice cream from the root beer float she was drinking, and listened with contentment to the chatter around her. The group had settled at one of the big round tables in the back of the Dairi Burger, one of the most popular places in town. A jukebox with a selection of current hits was part of its appeal, as well as a big game room with the latest video games and two dilapidated pinball machines. It was a perfect place to meet after a day at the beach, and as Elizabeth smiled around the table at the group of classmates she and Jeffrey had joined, she could feel herself relaxing.

She had woken up that morning still angry with Jessica. Her sister's cavalier attitude toward the mishap the night before was what had irritated her the most. OK, so Jessica had made a mistake. That seemed fair enough, though it was hardly an isolated occurrence. The least Jessica could have done was to take the mistake seriously, Elizabeth thought. Instead she had brushed it off, acting surprised that Elizabeth even cared.

But Elizabeth had decided by midmorning to try her hardest to forget Jessica and enjoy her day with Jeffrey instead. She couldn't help feeling that things had been slightly strained between them since the night she had been forced to cancel their date at Tiberino's. Also, one or both of them had been so busy lately! They had had fun playing tennis the day before, but it hadn't been very personal. They hadn't had a close talk in ages!

But today . . . today had been absolutely perfect, Elizabeth thought happily, taking a sip of root beer. They had found a deserted little cove miles down the public beach and had spread out their towels, lying down and holding hands as the sun beat down and the waves crashed in. She blushed a little, remembering some of the affectionate things Jeffrey had said. Her reverie was interrupted by Winston Egbert, who was being his usual boisterous self. A straw wrapper whizzed past her.

"Warning! Warning! Twin approaching!" Winston shrieked, pretending to duck.

Elizabeth laughed. Sure enough, Jessica was hurrying toward the crowded table.

"Sorry I'm late, everyone!" Jessica exclaimed, taking the chair next to Jeffrey that they'd been saving for her.

"We've been frantic," Winston said with mock concern. "We thought you'd been abducted. Or drawn and quartered. Or at least triviaed out."

Jessica rolled her eyes at him. "Thanks for your concern, Winston," she said wryly. Everyone laughed at this exchange, and Jessica fished around in her handbag, leaning past Jeffrey to pass Elizabeth the folded piece of paper.

"What's this?" Elizabeth asked, surprised.

"Todd called," Jessica said. "You know, he wanted to talk about Friday night."

To her dismay, Elizabeth felt herself turning red. Jeffrey was looking at her quizzically, and she glanced away, a funny feeling in her stomach. The truth was that she still hadn't gotten around to talking to Jeffrey about Todd and the awards banquet. *Leave it to Jessica*, she thought. At least everybody else at the table was busy talking. No one seemed to have heard what Jessica said. No one, that is, but Jeffrey.

"Don't you want to know what he said?" Jessica demanded,

Elizabeth was still beet red. "What did he say?" she managed, trying to sound natural. Jeffrey was staring at her, and she felt terribly uncomfortable.

"Just that the dinner is still on for Friday and you should call him and let him know if you can still go."

"Thanks," Elizabeth said, toying with her spoon. "I'll explain in a minute," she murmured to Jeffrey.

Jeffrey was avoiding her gaze. "That's all right," he muttered. "Will you excuse me?" he said, pushing his chair back and getting to his feet. "I've got to take off. I just remembered I promised my mom I'd have the car back by six."

Elizabeth barely noticed the surprised objections everyone raised. She got up, too, determined to go with him. She knew Jeffrey wouldn't make a scene by telling her not to come with him. Hastily putting some money on the table to cover their part of the bill, she hurried after him.

"What was that all about?" she demanded. "Were you really planning on just storming out on me?"

89

Jeffrey's face was pale and his mouth tight with anger. "What's the deal, Liz? First you tell me Todd is coming in for the carnival. Then I find out *by accident* that you've got some kind of date lined up with him for Friday. What about *our* date? Weren't we supposed to go to the opening party together?"

They had crossed to the door now, and Elizabeth hurried after Jeffrey as he headed to his car. "I can't believe you!" she exclaimed. "Aren't you even going to give me a chance to explain?"

"You don't have to explain. Your face gave the whole thing away," he said bitterly, jerking the car door open and getting in the driver's seat.

"Jeffrey!" Elizabeth exclaimed. "For heaven's sake, will you let me—" She broke off, hurrying around to the passenger's side and getting in the car. She didn't want to risk his driving off before she could explain what had happened, and he seemed almost angry enough to do just that.

"Go on, then. Tell me what's up," he challenged.

Elizabeth bit her lip. "It really isn't a very big deal," she said slowly. "I'm just surprised by the way you're acting. You know Todd and I are friends. Why are you acting so jealous?''

"Maybe I *am* jealous," Jeffrey said. "Come on, Liz. Look at it from my point of view. Everyone always talks about what a great thing you and Todd had together. You two went out for ages. Can't you see why that would make me feel uncomfortable? Of course I feel insecure! I was worried about his being around for the carnival as it was. And then your sister starts saying things about Friday night like—" He broke off, looking really upset.

"Jeffrey, listen!" Elizabeth exclaimed. "I didn't tell you earlier because I was hoping the awards dinner would be changed to another night, and I really would prefer to go with you to the opening party." She explained about the awards dinner, and Jeffrey's expression softened. "Anyway, it's hardly a big deal. Todd wants me to go because I know Timothy, the boy who's getting the scholarship. It's honestly not anything to be jealous of, Jeffrey—an awards banquet sponsored by the PTA!"

Jeffrey looked sheepish. "Well, maybe I jumped to conclusions," he admitted. "But why didn't you mention it to me earlier?" he asked. *"That's* what bothers me, Liz. It makes it seem like you had something to hide."

Elizabeth frowned. "I told you. I didn't want to get you upset before I knew for sure that the banquet was definitely going to be held on Friday."

Jeffrey turned the key in the ignition. "Well, I don't know if I buy that," he muttered. "You could have mentioned it to me anyway. This way it all seems kind of sneaky and under-handed, Liz. How would you feel if the tables were turned?"

Elizabeth just stared at him. She honestly hadn't expected him to be this upset.

In fact, it bothered her a great deal to hear him talking this way. Maybe she should have mentioned the potential conflict earlier, but that was hardly an excuse for his behavior. Didn't she have a right to spend an evening with an old friend? Jeffrey could hardly expect her not to see Todd at all when he was back, could he?

It seemed to Elizabeth that Jeffrey was being unreasonable. It might have been flattering if he had been a tiny bit jealous, but this—this seemed ridiculous!

He was acting as if he owned her. As if the

entire world were going to collapse if she spent a minute alone with Todd.

Elizabeth felt confused and upset. She hardly knew what to say, and apparently Jeffrey didn't either. They rode the rest of the way back to the Wakefields' house in silence, and after a terse goodbye Elizabeth got out of the car, half expecting him to stop her before she reached the front walk.

But he didn't stop her. In fact, he pulled away at once, and Elizabeth felt a sinking sensation in the pit of her stomach as she watched his car disappear. Their wonderful day had turned into a disaster.

Now what was she going to do?

Nine

The phone ringing woke Elizabeth up Sunday morning. She started to reach for it, but it stopped. She looked at her clock and saw that it was almost time to get up. As she lay there, she thought about the evening before. It didn't seem possible it had really happened. Sitting up in bed, she stared unhappily at the sunlight streaming in through her open window. Everything rushed back to her, and her eyes filled with tears. How could Jeffrey have acted the way he had? Didn't he trust her at all? Maybe she should have mentioned the dinner with Todd as soon as it came up, but it was hardly as though she'd been scheming.

She cared a great deal for Todd, but they were friends now, nothing more.

Sighing, Elizabeth swung her legs over the side of her bed and got up. She headed mechanically over to her dresser and picked up her hairbrush, frowning at her reflection. She wasn't sure what she ought to do. It didn't seem to be up to her to call and apologize, but from the angry expression on Jeffrey's face the night before, it was unlikely that he would be the first to call.

They had planned to spend the afternoon together with a big group at a picnic at Secca Lake, but Elizabeth wasn't certain now that he would show up. Feeling terrible, she set her hairbrush down.

"Liz? Can I come in?" Jessica called, flying in before Elizabeth could respond. "It's gorgeous out!" Jessica declared, twisting her hair up into a high ponytail as she spoke and twirling around in a little half-circle. "What a great day for a picnic! Liz, do you realize this is your lucky day. David just called, and he says he's going to meet us all at the lake."

"I thought you hated David," Elizabeth said absently.

"I don't really *hate* him," Jessica admitted, tilting her head to one side as she considered the matter. "I think he's a jerk for taking the 'Trivia Bowl' so seriously, but he *is* kind of cute. Besides, Amy and I talked it over last night, and we're sure the two of us can go to work on him and get him to change his mind."

Elizabeth pulled open a dresser drawer and frowned at its contents. She really wasn't in a very good mood for a picnic. What if Jeffrey just didn't come at all? What if he never spoke to her again?

"Hey, what's wrong?" Jessica asked. "You seem really upset."

Elizabeth looked long and hard at her sister. Why not ask Jessica's advice? This time it really wasn't Jessica's fault that things had gone awry. Jessica had done only what Elizabeth had made her promise to do—take a careful phone message and deliver it promptly. Maybe she hadn't shown the greatest tact in announcing it in front of Jeffrey, but then Jessica had no way of knowing that Elizabeth hadn't told him about the awards banquet.

"It's Jeffrey," she said helplessly. "Jess, he's really mad at me because of Todd." Taking a deep breath, she proceeded to fill her sister in on everything that had happened the night before. Jessica listened thoughtfully.

"Hmmm," she said at last, plopping down in the chair to think it over. "Has Jeffrey ever acted possessive of you before?"

Elizabeth shook her head unhappily. "Never. Of course, I haven't really given him any reason to before. Not that I have now," she added hastily. "But you know what I mean."

"Of course," Jessica said reassuringly. "You know, I don't think this is such a big deal," she added. "I mean, my experience has always been that it doesn't hurt to make a guy a little jealous. Now that you and Jeffrey have been going out pretty seriously for a while, you're just at the stage when things are in danger of getting boring. Maybe Jeffrey needs something like this to keep him from taking you for granted."

Elizabeth thought this over. "But he's never taken me for granted," she objected.

"Well, he may have been on the verge of it before this thing with Todd came up." Jessica's eyes sparkled. "I think you're lucky, Liz. With Todd coming, you can make sure Jeffrey realizes how special you are. I wouldn't take it too far or anything, but a few moments of insecurity never did anyone any harm."

Elizabeth looked wonderingly at her. "So what do you think I should do?"

"I wouldn't do anything. Are you going to see Jeffrey today?"

"I was *supposed* to. We were going to meet up at Secca Lake with everyone else. But I was thinking I should call him to make sure he's still planning on coming. The way we left things last night . . ." Elizabeth's voice trailed off.

"Don't call him," Jessica advised. "Just go to the picnic and act perfectly normal. Let *him* do the apologizing. Remember what that dating book said, the one Mom gave us years ago that we used to crack up over? 'It never hurts to let a boy worry a little.' Not bad advice, really."

Elizabeth smiled. She remembered the book. She, Amy, and Jessica used to laugh themselves sick over it. "Well, maybe you're right," she mused. "Jeffrey really was being kind of unfair about the whole thing."

"Of course he was! It's because he's just realizing how madly in love with you he is. I'm telling you, Liz, with a little careful planning you'll have him wrapped around your little finger. I can just see the two of you at the Snow Ball," she added rapturously.

"You and Jeffrey will be dancing together, and suddenly he'll see Todd coming toward you. He'll get all protective of you. He'll hold you really close and start telling you how much he loves you. Poor Todd will be stricken," she added gleefully. "It'll be fantastic!"

Elizabeth laughed out loud. "I don't know, Jess. I don't think I could really enjoy having two guys fighting over me."

Jessica shook her head impatiently. "You just don't give yourself enough credit," she protested. "Trust me, Liz. Don't try too hard to put Jeffrey's mind at ease. A little dose of jealousy is just what he needs. Follow my advice, and you'll be the hit of the Snow Ball. I promise!"

Elizabeth grinned. "Well, it's worth a try. Anyway, it sounds like all you're advising me to do is play it cool for the next few days. And *that* can't possibly get me into trouble!"

"That's the spirit," Jessica said warmly. "Come on. We've got to get ready for the picnic," she added.

Jessica had been looking forward to the afternoon anyway, but now that she had the prospect of watching Elizabeth and Jeffrey in action, she could hardly wait for the picnic to get started!

*   *   *

By three o'clock the picnic was in full swing. About twenty-five juniors had gathered by the lake, and bright blankets had been spread out and heaped with sandwiches and cold drinks. Ken Matthews and Bill Chase had both brought tape decks, and the air was filled with music. Jessica was trying to organize Frisbee softball on the flat meadow near the lake, and Elizabeth and Enid were watching with amusement from the sidelines as Caroline Pearce went to "bat" with the fluorescent disk.

"Where's Jeffrey?" Enid asked her friend. "I thought you two were coming together."

Elizabeth pretended to be deeply absorbed in the ice-cream sandwich she was unwrapping. "I guess he's coming later. I don't know," she said in an offhand voice.

Enid's green eyes widened. "Uh-oh. Did something happen that I don't know about?"

Elizabeth shrugged. "Not really, except Jeffrey turns out to have a real jealous streak." She filled her friend in on the events of the day before, and Enid listened with concern.

"I don't know if I agree with Jessica's advice," she said finally. "Jeffrey really strikes me as sensitive. Don't you think it would be better to tell him how you feel, to make sure he understands that it's all over between you and Todd?"

Elizabeth flushed. Secretly she had wondered the same thing herself when Jessica was talking to her that morning. But now she felt defensive about her strategy. "He ought to know that. I've made it pretty clear," she objected. "Speaking of the devil," she added as she spotted Jeffrey strolling across the meadow from the parking lot. Her stomach did flip-flops when she saw him. He was *so* cute, especially in the faded madras pants he was wearing. She loved the way his hair glinted in the sunlight. Suddenly she felt herself melt. She wanted nothing more than to run to him, throw her arms around him, and apologize for the night before.

But the next instant she caught Jessica's eye. Jessica was standing on the makeshift pitcher's mound, waving the Frisbee toward her sister. Jeffrey was between them now, walking toward Elizabeth and Enid. When Jessica gave her sister a victory sign with her fingers, Elizabeth felt her resolve returning. Jessica was right. It was terribly important to make Jeffrey understand that he couldn't treat her the way he had the day before. She had promised to play it cool, and she was going to, even if it seemed to go against her intuition.

"Liz, can I talk to you?" Jeffrey said, coming directly to the spot where Enid and Elizabeth were sitting.

"Sure," Elizabeth said, making it sound as if nothing out of the ordinary had happened. "We'll be back in a second," she told Enid, who was looking on with an amused expression on her face.

"I felt terrible about last night," Jeffrey said in a low voice as they walked toward the lake.

"Oh, last night," Elizabeth said in an artificial voice. Her heart went out to him, and she wanted to give up the game-playing right away. But she had promised Jessica she'd try.

"I was just really hurt that you hadn't told me about this dinner thing before. I guess it's kind of hard for me. I mean, I've never had a serious girlfriend before. And you and Todd . . ."

"That's true," Elizabeth said, taking a deep breath. "Todd and I have really shared an awful lot."

Jeffrey looked miserable. "I bet you two still care for each other, too," he muttered, kicking a pebble into the water.

"Well," Elizabeth said, trying for the right mixture of remote tenderness, "I guess we do, really. I mean, after you've been through everything Todd and I have— Well, you're bound to still feel *something*. I wouldn't be human if I didn't, right?"

"Yeah," Jeffrey said shortly. "Yeah, I guess so."

"Let's just forget all about it for now," Elizabeth said. She smiled at him. "We can talk about it some other time, can't we? It's a gorgeous day."

Jeffrey looked distraught. "I've got this awful feeling that you're hiding something from me, Liz. You're not acting like yourself."

Remember, Elizabeth told herself—*mysterious and remote*. If she was going to keep Jeffrey feeling jealous, she couldn't be too reassuring. "I'm not hiding anything," she declared, averting her eyes just enough to make herself look a little guilty.

"Liz, I want to know right now how you feel about Todd," Jeffrey said loudly. "I can't stand this! Are you still in love with him or what?"

"Of course I'm not still in love with him," Elizabeth said reprovingly. "But I can care for him anyway, can't I?"

103

"I don't like the idea of sharing you, that's all," he retorted. "And I don't like the way you're talking about all of this, either. I don't think you're being straight with me. And it isn't like you."

"I'm being completely honest about everything," Elizabeth told him hastily. "Come on, Jeffrey," she added, trying hard for a Jessica-like pout. "Let's stop arguing and just relax and have a good time. Why don't we go up and play Frisbee with everyone?"

"I don't feel like playing Frisbee," Jeffrey snapped, pulling away from her. "I'm going to go get a sandwich," he added, storming up the bank toward Enid.

Elizabeth stood there, feeling terrible. Something told her that this wasn't the way things were supposed to have gone. Either she wasn't very good at making guys jealous, or Jessica's plan wasn't the best.

She didn't seem to have done much to straighten things out. "Great," she muttered to herself, climbing up the bank to join Enid.

The truth was that she had made a little mess into a bigger mess. And she couldn't help feeling that it was partly Jessica's fault—again.

Ten

It was Tuesday morning, and Elizabeth and Enid were standing and talking at Enid's locker before school began. "You mean he hasn't called you since *Sunday*?" Enid demanded incredulously. "That doesn't seem like Jeffrey!"

"Well, we bumped into each other this morning, and he asked me if I'd meet him in the cafeteria at noon," Elizabeth said unhappily. "He didn't look like himself. In fact, he seemed really on edge. I just hope I haven't completely messed everything up. I don't think Jessica's advice worked in our case.

Jeffrey just doesn't seem like the kind of guy who enjoys being jealous."

Enid's green eyes were emphatic. "Of course not! No offense to your sister, but I think this game-playing nonsense is for the birds. Jeffrey's above that sort of thing, and I'm sure he thinks you are, too. He probably figures if you're trying to make him jealous, you've got a pretty good reason for it." She looked closely at her friend. "You *don't* still feel anything for Todd, do you?"

Elizabeth laughed. "No, I don't," she told Enid. "I may be confused, but I'm not *that* confused. I just don't think it's fair for Jeffrey to demand that I give up my friendship with Todd. What do you think?"

Enid looked serious. "I think you have to be very sensitive. I mean, you're absolutely right as far as the principle of the thing is concerned. In theory Jeffrey is being overpossessive. But look at it from his point of view. He really needs a lot of reassurance from you, Liz. I just hope . . ."

"What?" Elizabeth demanded as her friend's voice trailed off.

"I just hope it all works out," Enid said. She gave Elizabeth a warm smile. "I'm sure it will, too. You two have so much going for you.

You're not going to let a dumb argument wreck everything now."

Just then the bell rang. Elizabeth and Enid had to go in separate directions. "I'll let you know what happens," Elizabeth said dejectedly as she walked away.

"I've been feeling absolutely rotten since Sunday afternoon," Jeffrey began, his eyes fixing seriously on Elizabeth's. They were sitting opposite each other at one of the tables on the patio outside the cafeteria.

Elizabeth swallowed. "I've felt horrible, too," she admitted in a low voice.

"Liz, we've got to straighten this out!" Jeffrey added in an anguished voice. "I feel like I'm losing you!"

Elizabeth stared at him, her lips trembling slightly. "I feel terrible about the way I acted on Sunday afternoon. The last thing I meant was to make you think I'm still the slightest bit interested in Todd. Nothing could be further from the truth. It's *you* I care about, Jeffrey. You should know that by now!"

Jeffrey reached across the table to clasp her hands tightly in his. "That makes me so happy," he said sincerely. "So does this mean you'll come with me to the opening party on Friday night?"

Elizabeth blinked. This wasn't what she had expected him to say at all. "I don't know," she said uncomfortably. "I haven't spoken to Todd yet, but I'll probably talk to him either tonight or tomorrow night." She looked away, not really sure what to say to him. "Is it really such a big deal?" she asked at last. "I mean this awards banquet is for such a good cause. And it would mean a lot to Todd for me to go with him."

"What about what it means to me to have you with me on Friday night?"

Elizabeth pulled her hands from his. She was starting to get angry. "Jeffrey, you're not being fair!" she exclaimed. "Todd's only going to be here for a few days. It would be different if you had some reason to suspect I still felt something for him, but I promise you, I don't. He's just a good friend!"

"Well, then that means I should get priority on Friday night," Jeffrey objected. "You and I have been planning on going to the carnival together for weeks, Liz. This awards banquet thing seems to have just come up out of the blue."

"It *didn't* just come up out of the blue,"

Elizabeth said hotly, her eyes filling with tears. "Jeffrey, come on! It's not like missing the party on Friday night is going to ruin our whole weekend. I'll drive up Saturday morning, and we'll still have the rest of the weekend together."

"Great," Jeffrey said moodily, slumping in his chair. "And I suppose Todd will just happen to not have a date for the Snow Ball, so he'll have to spend the whole night dancing with you!"

Elizabeth's face was flushed with anger. "You're being impossible!" she snapped. "For goodness' sake, Jeffrey, you're acting like a three-year-old. Can't you stop being selfish and jealous for just a second and realize that going to the awards banquet is completely reasonable."

"It *isn't* reasonable," Jeffrey said furiously. "You're *my* girlfriend, right? Not Todd's. You and I had plans for Friday night, and now you're trying to break them. *That* isn't reasonable!"

Elizabeth jumped up from the table, so furious she was shaking. "If you're going to act like this, I'm *glad* I'm going to the awards banquet with Todd instead of that stupid party with you."

"I'm glad, too," Jeffrey said loudly, as angry as she was. "Why don't you just spend the whole *weekend* with Todd, if you feel that way about him?"

"Maybe I will!" Elizabeth sputtered, tears running down her cheeks. "He's a lot better company than you are. I can tell you that much!" As soon as those words were out of her mouth, she regretted them, but she was far too angry to apologize. Spinning on her heel, she ran from the patio.

But she couldn't put the impression of Jeffrey's anguished face out of her mind. She knew her parting retort had stung him terribly. It was one of the worst afternoons she could remember, and all she could do was suffer through one class after another, praying for it to end so she could escape and be by herself.

It seemed that the final bell signaling that the day was over would never come. But at last it did, and Elizabeth made her way through the crowded halls to her locker. She felt numb—as if her feelings had been erased and all she could do was let herself be propelled by the crowd around her. Before she reached her locker, she was accosted by Amy Sutton and Jessica, who were beside themselves with excitement.

"Liz, wish us luck. We're off to the station!" Jessica sang out, dancing happily around her sister. She was oblivious of Elizabeth's stony expression.

"Good luck," Elizabeth muttered.

"Do we look all right?" Amy asked, smoothing down the front of the black sweater and houndstooth skirt she was wearing and twirling around for Elizabeth's inspection.

"You look fine," Elizabeth said, reaching her locker and noting with some surprise that a piece of notebook paper had been folded and stuck in one of the metal slots just at eye level. Maybe it was a note from Jeffrey.

"If we win today this could be the beginning of really big things," Jessica was exclaiming excitedly. She and Amy were in such high spirits it was hard to imagine their being able to sit still for the duration of the contest. But Elizabeth wasn't paying attention to them. Fingers trembling, she unfolded the note. Sure enough, it was from Jeffrey.

I'm driving out to Las Palmas Canyon this afternoon to think things through. I'll be there until six. If you want to talk, meet me at the intersection of Route 27 and Canyon Drive. If you don't come, I'll assume the worst.

That was the whole note. It was signed "Jeffrey," not "love," just "Jeffrey." Elizabeth scanned the note several times before turning urgently to her sister. "What time are you going to be back with the car?"

"The show only lasts half an hour. It starts at three-thirty, so I should be home by four-thirty at the latest. Why? Is anything wrong?"

Elizabeth thought quickly. If Jessica had the car back by four-thirty, she could make it to the canyon by five o'clock. "You promise you'll have it back by four-thirty? It's an emergency," she said quietly. "I really need you to promise, Jess."

"I promise," Jessica said soberly, her eyes wide.

"Jess, *come on*. We're going to be late," Amy whined.

Sighing, Elizabeth turned to her locker. She hoped Jessica kept her word this time. Because from the sound of Jeffrey's note, if she didn't make it out to the canyon, it was going to be the end of everything between them.

She was still angry about everything that had happened, but she didn't want to lose him. She had to do her best to get out to Las Palmas Canyon by six o'clock.

The excitement was mounting in the television studio. On one side of the dais Jake Thomas and David Campbell were sitting, their faces tense as the questions came thicker and faster. Jessica and Amy were sitting on the other side of the dais while Mike Malloy, the host of "Trivia Bowl," fired questions. For the first half of the show, Jake and David had been in the lead, but in the second half Amy and Jessica had caught up. Now it was the last question, and the score was tied.

"OK, folks, this is it," Mike Malloy boomed, "the question that determines which team has the chance to appear on the live version of 'Trivia Bowl' that will be aired next month. Are you ready?"

"We're ready," David said tensely, avoiding Jessica's imploring gaze.

"OK, folks. Take a deep breath, think very, very hard, and here's the question. Remember, ladies, it goes to Jake and David first. And the question is: How many fluid cups are there in a gallon? I repeat: How many fluid cups in a gallon?"

"Oh, nooooo," Jessica groaned. She couldn't believe how easy the question was—after they'd been stumped for the last twenty-five minutes on really tough questions! They knew they had lost now.

"I've got it!" David announced, snapping his fingers. "Twenty-four," he said triumphantly, sitting back in his chair and grinning.

"Twenty-four cups is absolutely—wrong," Mike Malloy said. "OK, folks, that means the question goes to the other team. It's a tie-breaker! Can either of you girls tell me how many fluid cups there are in one gallon?"

"Sixteen!" Jessica and Amy shrieked in unison.

"Sixteen is *right*! Jessica and Amy, you're our first winners!" Mike yelled above their excited laughter.

For the next few moments pandemonium broke out in the studio. Amy and Jessica were so excited they were practically hysterical. Jessica even hugged David in her excitement, and he hugged her back. "Nice work," he said, kissing her on the cheek.

"This calls for a celebration," Mike said. "What do you say we go for pizza at the Pizza Palace?"

"That sounds wonderful!" Jessica exclaimed. "I'll drive," she assured Amy, squeezing her arm with a smile on her face.

It was four thirty-five, but Jessica didn't notice the clock. As usual, she wasn't wearing a watch, and she had lost track of the time.

She had also completely forgotten her promise to Elizabeth.

Eleven

Elizabeth was pacing back and forth in the Wakefields' living room, looking nervously at her watch. It was a little after four-thirty, and Jessica still wasn't back. *She said the show would be over by four o'clock,* Elizabeth thought anxiously. *So where is she?*

For what must have been the dozenth time she went to the window and looked down the street, hoping to see the Fiat. But there were no cars driving by. What if Jeffrey wasn't there when she showed up? What if he had changed his mind and decided he never wanted to talk to her again? After what she'd said . . .

Elizabeth cringed every time she remembered her parting words that day at lunch. How could she have been so cruel? Enid was right. Jeffrey was just a sensitive, caring guy. So maybe he *was* a little possessive. Wasn't that better than if he didn't care about her at all?

She felt awful. The truth was that she loved Jeffrey very much. It had taken her a long time to realize that, but she did.

Now Elizabeth was facing the difficult truth that she might be grappling with the problem of divided loyalties. Maybe she *did* still feel something for Todd. She knew in her heart that any romantic attachment she had ever had to him was gone, but she felt she still owed him some kind of special loyalty. Had she been wrong to assume that the banquet with Todd ought to take precedence over the opening-night festivities at Mont Blanc?

All Elizabeth knew now was that she needed to talk everything out with Jeffrey. "Only this time we really need to talk," she said aloud. "Not accuse each other or shout at each other, but really *talk*." She looked nervously at her watch. Quarter to five and no sign of Jessica. The canyon was at least a thirty-minute ride—unless Jessica was back soon she was going to risk missing him.

A few minutes later Elizabeth had looked up the number of the television station where the "Trivia Bowl" was taking place and was on the phone. She wasn't going to let her twin mess things up again. If Jessica wasn't on her way home already, Elizabeth was going to let her have it!

To her annoyance, the receptionist kept her on the phone for ages. First she put Elizabeth on hold, then started to ask what she wanted, and then put her on hold again. Finally Elizabeth was allowed to ask her question. "I'm looking for a girl named Jessica Wakefield. She was a contestant in the 'Trivia Bowl' competition this afternoon," she explained. "Is she still in the studio, or has she gone home?"

"Just a minute," the receptionist said curtly. She was away for what seemed ages, and Elizabeth fidgeted and glanced at her watch. Five o'clock already! What on earth could the receptionist be doing?

"I'm very sorry, but she isn't here," the woman said at last, sounding as though it were all Elizabeth's fault. "They've all gone to celebrate at some restaurant. Would you like to leave a message?"

Elizabeth blinked. "They've gone to a restaurant?'' she repeated dully. She couldn't believe her ears. "Do you know which restaurant?" she asked, fighting to stay calm.

"Sorry," the receptionist said. "I have no way of knowing."

"Thanks," Elizabeth said, hanging the phone up with trembling fingers. She couldn't believe it. How could Jessica do this to her?

It was five after five. Unless she could find a car to borrow in the next twenty minutes, there was no point in trying to meet Jeffrey. His note had made it clear that he would wait for her only until six o'clock. Shaking with anger and anxiety, Elizabeth dialed Enid's number.

"Liz? Is anything wrong?" Enid asked sleepily. "I was just taking a nap . . ."

"Enid, is there any way I could borrow your mom's car? I know it's an incredible imposition, but I have a crisis and Jess has the Fiat, and neither of my parents are at home, and I need to meet Jeffrey at Las Palmas Canyon in the next half hour."

Enid sounded more alert. "Oh, no. My mom has the car, Liz. She was going to run some errands after work. I don't think she'll be back for a while."

Elizabeth felt her eyes fill with tears. "OK, Enid. Thanks anyway."

"Are you all right? What's going on?"

"I'll call you back later," Elizabeth promised. "I'm going to see if I can borrow a car from one of the neighbors."

She hung up, blinking tears back. She realized that it was pointless to try to borrow a car. Most of the neighbors wouldn't be home from work yet.

The only thing she could think of now was calling a cab company. She had no idea how much it would cost to take a taxi all the way to Las Palmas Canyon, but she was desperate. If she didn't show up, Jeffrey was going to think it was all over between them. He'd never talk to her again. Tears were spilling over now as she flipped through the yellow pages. She called the first cab company she came across and falteringly asked how much a ride to the canyon would cost.

"It'd run you about thirty dollars," the man told her.

Thirty dollars! Elizabeth's heart sank. She knew she didn't have that much cash. In fact, she was sure she didn't have more than ten dollars. Mrs. Wakefield kept fifteen dollars in a canister in the kitchen for emergencies, but even if she could justify this as a family emergency, that wouldn't cover the cost. But the man put an end to her speculation anyway. "We won't be able to send a cab out there for at least an hour, though," he told her. "Rush hour just started, and we can't spare a car that long."

Elizabeth hung up in a daze. It was five-fifteen. The thought of Jeffrey standing at the intersection, watching hopefully as each car whizzed past, was heartbreaking. She would never forgive her sister. Never! Nothing Jessica had done in the past compared to this. Elizabeth felt she was going to explode with anger. She was certain she would never talk to her sister again.

And the way things were looking now, Jeffrey was never going to talk to *her* again. Elizabeth felt as though her entire world were collapsing, and all she could do was sit there and watch it crumble around her.

"Liz? Are you in here?" Jessica called, opening the back door and hurrying across the kitchen. The house was dark and quiet, and there was no sign of her sister anywhere.

Jessica turned the light on when she got to

the living room and jumped in surprise. Elizabeth was sitting on the couch in the dark, staring straight at her. Jessica couldn't believe how strange she looked. Her face was expressionless, but her eyes looked stormy.

"Liz, you're never going to believe what happened—we won!" Jessica exclaimed. "Amy and I won! We get to be on the first live, televised 'Trivia Bowl.' And you'll never guess the question that broke the tie," she added, giggling as she remembered.

Elizabeth just stared at her, not saying a word.

"Is something wrong?" Jessica asked, worried. She couldn't remember ever seeing her sister look this way before.

"Jess, what time is it?" Elizabeth said in a flat, tired voice.

"It's—" Jessica frowned at the clock on the wall. "Uh, six o'clock," she said. She paled a little. "Was I supposed to make dinner tonight? I thought—"

"The car, Jess," Elizabeth said. "Don't you remember promising me that you'd have the car back by four-thirty?"

Jessica stared at her, stricken. "Omigod!" She gasped, clapping her hand to her mouth. "Liz, I completely forgot! I don't believe this. I swear, I just totally forgot all about it. We were so excited about winning, and Mike Malloy wanted to treat all four of us to pizza. Liz, will you ever forgive me? What did you need the car for? Is it too late now?"

Elizabeth stared coldly at her twin. "Jeffrey and I have been fighting ever since I followed the advice you gave me on Sunday. Today was the worst. We had a huge argument at lunch, and after school I found this note in my locker." She passed it to her sister. "I don't know how important it seems to *you*, but it seems pretty major to me."

Jessica read the note hastily, her face draining of color. "Wow," she whispered. "I've really messed things up, haven't I?"

Elizabeth just stared at her. "Well, so much for Jeffrey and me," she said at last, getting up and walking out of the room. She was too angry with her sister to say another word. She just wanted to be alone.

Jessica stared down at Jeffrey's note, her eyes darkening with concern. "Liz, *wait*," she exclaimed, hurrying after her. "You have to talk to me! Isn't there some way to explain that it was my fault you didn't make it out to the canyon in time? Can't you tell him and—"

"Jess," Elizabeth interrupted stonily, "the

next time I want your advice I'll ask for it. OK?"

"OK," Jessica said, stung by her sister's words.

"I've had it!" Elizabeth cried, tears spilling down her cheeks. "Jess, you have absolutely no consideration for me—no respect for my feelings. You would never treat a friend the way you treat me. Well, I'm sick and tired of it. I've asked you over and over again to have the decency, the common courtesy, to keep your promises, to listen to me when I ask you for a favor. This afternoon I realized that this is it. I just can't trust you anymore, Jess." She spun on her heel and stomped upstairs, leaving Jessica staring after her.

Twelve

By nine o'clock that evening Jessica had come
up with a plan to make Elizabeth forgive her.
In fact, she couldn't help feeling proud of herself when she looked back over the events of
that day. She had actually managed to win the
"Trivia Bowl" without David's help—and had
managed not to antagonize him, either, which
was miraculous. By eight o'clock she had
taken a bubble bath, done the dishes—a generous gesture, as it was Elizabeth's turn—and
finished her French homework. That left the
rest of the evening free to talk on the phone to
Cara Walker.

Cara had always been one of Jessica's best

friends, but they hadn't seen much of each other recently, especially since Jessica and Amy had gotten involved in the trivia show. Now it seemed they had tons to catch up on. Cara had been going out with the twins' older brother, Steven, for some time now, and it was clear that she was counting the minutes till she saw him again during Winter Carnival weekend.

"I can't wait. My mom got me a beautiful dress. It's strapless and glittery. Very ice-age," Cara said with a giggle. "I just hope Steve likes it."

"Steve would like anything you wore." Jessica laughed. "Hey, Cara, I need to ask your advice about something," she said, turning serious. She was in her favorite telephone position, lying on her stomach across the bed, ankles crossed in the air above her, and her chin propped up on one hand. "I'm in a real mess with Liz, and I need your advice on how to straighten it all out." She proceeded to fill Cara in on everything that had happened, and Cara listened sympathetically.

"Poor Liz!" she exclaimed when she had heard Jessica out. "Jess, it sounds to me as though you really screwed things up! No wonder she's mad."

126

This wasn't exactly what Jessica wanted to hear. "Oh, I know I can smooth everything over between her and Jeffrey," she said quickly. "I'm not really worried about *that*."

"Uh-oh," Cara said. "If I know you, Jess, the cure can be worse than the disease. What exactly are you planning to do?"

Jessica cleared her throat defensively. Actually, she didn't really have a coherent scheme. That was partly why she had called Cara. But she didn't want to seem unprepared. "I just have to talk to Todd, that's all," she said, thinking fast. "As soon as he realizes what a mess he's making of Liz's love life, I'm sure he'll tell her not to bother to come along on Friday night. Then she'll be free to join Jeffrey at the opening party at the lodge, and the trouble will be over."

"How are you going to find Todd before he talks to Elizabeth?" Cara asked skeptically.

"Oh, that's simple," Jessica said airily. "Liz told me he's staying at the Egberts'." Todd usually stayed either with Winstons' family or Ken Matthews's family when he came to visit.

"So what?"

"So," Jessica said, twisting the phone cord, "all I have to do is call Winston, find out what time Todd is coming, and make sure I'm the first person he sees when he gets here."

"Well, if anyone can do it, you can," Cara said admiringly. "I just hope for Liz's sake it all works," she added anxiously. "The carnival won't be much fun if she and Jeffrey aren't together."

"They'll be together," Jessica promised. "I got her into this mess, Cara. The least I can do is get her out of it!"

Actually, Jessica was proud of this scheme. The more she thought about it the better it sounded. And it was so simple, too. Jessica felt certain that all it would take were a few heavy hints for Todd to realize he was putting Elizabeth on the spot by asking her to go with him to that silly awards banquet.

"Winston?" Jessica said in her most friendly, charming voice when she called him later that evening. "It's me, Jessica. I'm just calling to tell you Amy and I won today! I knew you'd want to know since you're such an *expert* at trivia."

Winston coughed modestly. "Congratulations," he said. "It's nice of you to let me know, Jess."

128

"By the way," Jessica said, as if the thought had just struck her, "isn't Todd coming to stay with you this week?"

"Yeah. He's coming tomorrow, in fact. Why?"

"Oh, I just wanted to come over and say hello," Jessica said casually. "What time is he supposed to get to your house?"

"Well, his flight gets in around three. He should be here by four or four-thirty."

"Why don't the three of us go to the Dairi Burger, for old times sake?" Jessica suggested. "Wouldn't that be nice? A kind of 'welcome back' hamburger party."

"That sounds great, Jess," Winston said, delighted. "That's really a nice idea!"

It sure is, Jessica thought happily as she replaced the receiver a few minutes later. She had no doubt that she'd be able to convince Todd that Friday night was a bad idea.

And after that, all she would have to do was wait for Elizabeth to come running to her with thanks and apologies for having doubted her twin for even one tiny second!

Everything on Wednesday went according to plan. Jessica, Todd, and Winston had just finished their burgers and were listening to a new song on the jukebox, relaxing and reminiscing about old times. Before long the conversation turned, naturally enough, to the carnival. Jessica made a point of emphasizing how much fun the opening party was going to be and how much everyone had been looking forward to going.

"I didn't realize it was such a big deal," Todd said, looking concerned. "Maybe I shouldn't have asked Elizabeth to come to the PTA awards banquet with me. Do you think she'll be missing out on a lot if she doesn't go up to Mont Blanc until Saturday?"

Winston was at the jukebox, fishing in his pocket for change, and Jessica decided this was as good a moment as any to start dropping some hints. "Liz agreed to go with you to the awards banquet?" she asked, perplexed. "You're kidding!" She pretended to mull this information over. Suddenly a look of comprehension broke over her face. "*That* explains everything," she said, taking a sip of her soda.

"Explains what?" Todd asked. "Jess, have I made some kind of mistake or something?"

Jessica shook her head quickly. "Oh, no. I was just thinking that this might explain why

Jeffrey and Liz have been on the outs this week."

Todd looked distressed. "You think Jeffrey's mad because Liz is coming to this banquet with me? I'd hate to be the cause of any sort of trouble between them."

"Well, I don't want to say one way or another," Jessica said coyly. "But I know they've been really upset with each other. And now that I think of it, it seems like Jeffrey has a point. The opening party is an awfully big deal, Todd. I guess Liz just feels kind of obligated to come with you."

"Maybe if I ask her—" Todd began.

"Oh, you know Liz," Jessica objected. "She'd never admit anything was wrong in a million years. She's so sensitive and thoughtful when it comes to things like this."

Todd looked upset. "What should I do, Jess? Should I just tell her I don't want her to go with me? Would that free her up to go with Jeffrey on Friday, the way she'd planned?"

"That's a great idea!" Jessica exclaimed, noticing that Winston was coming back to the table. "Let's drop it for now," she added in a low voice, putting her hand on his arm. "I'm sure the two of you will be able to straighten everything out."

Todd nodded, looking puzzled and distracted. Jessica couldn't help feeling triumphant. She was convinced she had everything under control now. All Todd had to do was be a gentleman and quietly back out, and Elizabeth would be free to spend Friday with Jeffrey—and everything would be back to normal again!

Elizabeth had been looking forward to seeing Todd, but she couldn't help feeling he was acting peculiar. It was Wednesday evening, and he had come by and asked her to take a walk with him. "We need to talk," he had told her, looking at her closely. "It's been ages, and I want to find out everything that's going on with you."

That had sounded all right, but once they actually began talking, Elizabeth noticed that Todd seemed tense. She kept feeling as if he were trying to find something out, but she couldn't tell what it was. "How's everything going at school? How's *The Oracle*?" he asked her.

"Fine," Elizabeth said, wishing she could

sound more convincing. "I guess things have been kind of . . . I don't know, I guess I've been a little down lately," she admitted finally. "Just the midwinter blahs. Everyone gets them from time to time, right?"

"Right," Todd said thoughtfully. "What about Jeffrey? Is everything still going well between the two of you?"

"Oh, things are all right," Elizabeth said noncommittally. The truth was that she and Jeffrey hadn't spoken—not since she'd failed to meet him at the canyon the night before. But she couldn't see any point in burdening Todd with that. He was in town for only a few days, and she wanted to help him have a good time. Besides, it seemed as if it would be wrong to confide in Todd. Uncertain as she was about how things stood, it didn't seem right to talk about Jeffrey to Todd. It seemed a betrayal of Jeffrey's confidence.

"This party on Friday night," Todd began, looking at her closely. "It's kind of a big deal, isn't it?"

"You mean the party up at Mont Blanc? It's not that big a deal," Elizabeth said quickly.

"Are you sure? Because I was thinking about it, and it seems kind of silly for you to come to the banquet. I mean, it isn't like you

133

were really all that involved in the program. Why don't you just go up to the lodge with everyone else on Friday afternoon? I'll come up Saturday, and we'll have plenty of time to see each other anyway."

Elizabeth colored. "Are you saying you don't want me to come with you on Friday?" she asked. She couldn't believe her ears. Here she'd gone and made a big issue out of her right to accompany Todd, and he didn't even want her to go with him after all! *It figures*, she thought bitterly. *First I lose Jeffrey because of Todd. And now Todd's telling me to get lost!*

"Well, if you really want to come—" Todd was saying doubtfully, not looking overjoyed at the prospect.

"If you want me to come, I want to come," Elizabeth said, feeling incredibly foolish and embarrassed.

"Let me think it over. Maybe I should sound Timmy out and see how he feels," Todd said, not meeting her gaze. "I just don't want to mess up your weekend."

Elizabeth didn't answer. She didn't see how her weekend could get any worse at this point, but she didn't see what good it would do to tell Todd the whole wretched story. It

134

was beginning to look as though she might end up going to Mont Blanc Friday evening after all, but it would be lonely up there if Jeffrey wasn't talking to her!

Thirteen

"There really doesn't seem to be any point in having classes this morning," Nora Dalton, the pretty young French teacher, teased her class. "Your heads are all in the clouds today!"

"In the mountains, actually," Winston said, grinning. "Mont Blanc!"

"I appreciate how excited you all are, but we still have to get through this material," Ms. Dalton declared, ignoring the groans from the front row. Ms. Dalton was a firm teacher despite her relaxed, easy-going nature, and the students knew she meant business. Elizabeth, bent over her notebook, wished she was feeling more a part of the holiday mood that seemed to have settled over the school that Friday morning. Not that she wasn't looking forward to the carnival, but everything was such a mess! Without much enthusiasm, she had made arrangements for getting up to the lodge. Students had their choice of going up on their own or taking one of the buses leaving from the school parking lot. The juniors and seniors were getting out early so that they would have time to go home and get their things, but Elizabeth had brought her duffel bag with her to school that morning so she could stay and catch up on some work at *The Oracle*. She and Jessica were planning on taking the bus from the lot. Since Todd had called the day before to announce that there was no point in Elizabeth's attending the awards banquet, she had no reason not to join her classmates.

Of course, there was still the problem of Jeffrey.

By now Elizabeth felt she'd been a prize idiot not to explain what had happened with the car on Tuesday as soon as it happened. She could have called Jeffrey that night and explained everything. Instead she had been embarrassed and upset and had let day after day drag by. Now she felt too stupid to go up to him and try to make sense out of everything. He would naturally wonder why she hadn't approached him earlier—and she had no excuse.

And now Todd didn't want her at the banquet! He hadn't even spoken directly to her the night before. He had just left a message with Mrs. Wakefield. And the message was very clear: Not only would it be all right for Elizabeth not to go to the banquet, but it would be best if she didn't. He hadn't even said why. Elizabeth was stung when she read the note her mother left on the kitchen counter for her. She couldn't help wondering if Todd was just trying to get out of spending the evening with her. It sure looked that way!

Well, she had managed to botch everything up pretty well. Elizabeth wished she could get more involved in the animated conversations among her classmates about what clothing people were bringing and who would be rooming with whom. But she just couldn't feel very involved. She knew when four o'clock rolled around that she'd be on the bus with everyone else. But she couldn't get excited about the carnival. Not when she was going without Jeffrey.

*　　*　　*

"How's your reconciliation plan going?" Cara Walker asked, falling in step beside Jessica when the fifth-period bell had released them from classes.

Jessica frowned. "It seems to have hit a temporary snag," she admitted. "I didn't count on the fact that Elizabeth and Jeffrey are so completely inept when it comes to making up. You wouldn't believe the way they're avoiding each other! You'd think this dumb misunderstanding was something really serious!"

"But your scheme worked. Todd told Liz not to go with him to the banquet tonight, right?"

"Right. Only things are really awful now. Liz isn't going to the banquet, and she still isn't talking to Jeffrey! Which is why I've decided to take things into my own hands from now on. Those two are just too slow for their own good," Jessica added, her eyes twinkling.

"What are you going to do?" Cara asked, intrigued. They had stopped by a row of lockers, and Jessica was taking a spiral notebook out of her backpack and pulling the cap off a pen.

139

"I'm forging a note," Jessica said cheerfully. "If I don't write to Jeffrey and try to patch things up, no one will!"

Holding her notebook against a locker, she began to print in her best imitation of her sister's printing.

> Dear Jeffrey:
> I'm so sorry about the way I acted this week. Am I too late, or would you be willing to spend the evening with me tonight after all? I've realized I was a complete idiot. You were right. The carnival is a million times more important than any dumb banquet with Todd. Please forgive me. Let's meet at the ski lodge tonight at six-thirty. We can straighten things out then.
> Love,
> Liz

"There!" Jessica exclaimed, folding the sheet of paper and sticking it in the crack in Jeffrey's locker. "That ought to do it."

"Isn't Liz going to be annoyed when she finds out about this?" Cara asked as Jessica stuffed her notebook in her pack.

"Liz is so down right now that she can't

decide what's best for her. Luckily, I'm around to help her out. Once she and Jeffrey are finally back together, I'm sure she'll thank me. Besides, I can explain everything to her on the bus trip up."

Cara didn't look convinced. "I don't know, Jess. It seems to me—"

"Oh, look. There's Amy!" Jessica exclaimed. "Cara, I promised her I'd run over to The Ski Shop with her before we go home to pack. Amy wants to get a ski suit like mine, only in gold instead of silver."

"You two are going to look like robots." Cara giggled.

"Don't worry about Liz," Jessica added hastily, waving at her friend as she hurried down the hall. "Just worry about Steve and about what a fantastic time you two are going to have this weekend!"

As Jessica chased after Amy she couldn't help thinking that Cara was getting more like Steven as time wore on. In the old days Cara wouldn't have been so skeptical about a scheme that was so obviously foolproof!

Elizabeth was bound to be grateful for a little meddling when it came to a crisis like this. If Jessica didn't step in and save her twin's love life, there was no telling how long it would take before Jeffrey and Elizabeth got it together again.

"What do you think?" Amy asked, pivoting in front of the full-length mirror in The Ski Shop. The gold ski suit she had selected fit her perfectly. And with her blond hair and blue eyes, she looked sensational.

But Jessica was getting tired of shopping. They had already spent over an hour in the mall. Amy kept remembering things she needed—first, a bunch of miniature lotions and shampoos from the drugstore; then magazines and paperbacks for the bus trip; then tapes for her Walkman from the music store. It was taking ages.

The Ski Shop was their last stop, to Jessica's immense relief. It was already two-thirty, and they still had to get home, finish packing and be back at school in time for the four o'clock bus.

Carrying their packages, the girls made their way out to the parking lot and stashed everything in the trunk of the Fiat. "You're going to come back for me after you've finished packing, right?" Amy asked, taking a new tube of lipstick out of her makeup bag and putting it on, then checking it in the rearview mirror.

"Yeah, but you've got to be ready on time," Jessica said anxiously, putting the mirror back in position, then starting the car. "I don't want to miss the bus, Amy. I've got to talk to Liz on the way up to the lodge!"

"I won't be more than a couple of minutes," Amy exclaimed, offended. "All I have to do is throw a few things in a bag. Anyway," she added, "you're the one who usually runs about an hour behind schedule."

Jessica was frowning as she drove. It was just beginning to occur to her how sticky everything could get if she didn't have a chance to explain everything in advance to her sister.

Suppose Jeffrey found Elizabeth before Jessica could explain to her what she'd done?

Even worse, suppose Jessica and Amy missed the bus and *no one* was there to meet Jeffrey at the ski lodge at six-thirty? That was hardly going to help reconcile the quarreling couple! The more Jessica thought about it the trickier the whole thing seemed.

"What is it?" Amy asked. "You're awfully quiet all of a sudden."

"Just promise me you'll hurry," Jessica said

grimly, pulling the Fiat up to the Suttons' house. "I'm going to be back for you in *exactly* half an hour."

"OK, OK," Amy grumbled. She got out of the car and took her packages out of the trunk. She barely had time to close the door before Jessica had pulled out of the driveway with a squeal of tires, leaving her astonished friend staring after her.

By three-thirty Jessica was a wreck. She was pacing back and forth in Amy's bedroom, alternating between reproaches and pleas. "We've got to hurry!" she shrieked, then added a beseeching, "Please, Amy, can't you pack just a little bit more quickly?"

But neither approach seemed to help. Amy was flustered and upset, racing from her dresser to her closet and back to her bed again, where an enormous suitcase stood yawning open, already crammed with everything from a blow-dryer to electric curlers to thermal underwear and flannel nightgowns.

"You've got enough stuff in there to last three months," Jessica grumbled. "We're only going to be up there for three *days*, Amy."

But trying to rush Amy only worsened the

situation. She started forgetting where things were—her contact lens case, her toothbrush, her ski goggles, her special moisturizer that prevented windburn. Each of these items caused a separate crisis, several minutes of furious searching, and enormous relief, only to be followed by panic as the next item turned out to have vanished.

"Stop *pacing*," Amy begged, close to tears. "I'm moving as fast as I can, Jess. You're just making me nervous."

"Look," Jessica said, trying to be reasonable. "Why don't *I* go now and catch the bus, and you just follow in the car?"

Amy looked as though Jessica had just recommended suicide. "I can't drive your car!" she wailed. "I don't know how to use a stick shift. And besides, I can't see well in the dark. My contacts make headlights shimmer. I've got terrible night vision."

"And at this rate, we won't be leaving until dark," Jessica grumbled.

Finally Amy was packed and ready to go. "We can still make the bus," Jessica huffed, lugging one end of the enormous bag downstairs. It was three forty-five. With luck they could get to school in ten minutes and still have a minute or two to spare.

But luck wasn't on Jessica's side that afternoon. They hit every red light between Amy's house and the school. They also got stuck behind a stopped yellow school bus for several minutes; and the lights at the intersection just before Sweet Valley High were broken, causing a long delay while a policewoman tried to direct traffic. They were just about to turn into the school parking lot when Amy remembered that she'd forgotten her allergy pills. "Jess, I really need them," she whispered, looking sideways at Jessica with terror.

"OK, I give up. We'll go back and get your pills—and we'll just have to give up on the bus and drive up to Mont Blanc ourselves," Jessica said. "I'll have to let Liz know, though. She'll be really worried if I'm not on the bus." At the other end of the parking lot, she could see students milling around the buses, waiting to board. But she couldn't spot her twin.

Just then, a car horn beeped behind the Fiat. Looking in the rearview mirror, Jessica saw it was Sandra Bacon, one of the cheerleaders, and her mother. Jessica pulled the Fiat to the side to let them pass. Then she motioned for them to stop.

Sandra rolled down the car window. "What's up?"

146

"Sandra, will you do me a big favor and tell Liz that I won't be on the bus and that I'm driving up in the Fiat? Tell her I'll explain when I get there."

"Sure, no problem," Sandra said. "See you up there!" She waved as her mother started up the car again.

Jessica sighed. "OK, Amy, let's go get your pills." She turned the car around in the lot, then headed back toward Amy's house. On the way she explained about the note she had left for Jeffrey and her concern about missing Elizabeth.

"Oh, is that all?" Amy exclaimed, visibly relieved. "What's the big deal? All you have to do is catch Liz the minute we get up there." Looking considerably less guilty, she settled back in her seat. "I'm sure we'll beat the bus up there anyway!"

But not even Jessica's natural optimism could convince her that Amy was right. It seemed that there was a plot to prevent them from getting to the lodge on time. They had to stop for gas. Amy turned out to have dropped her keys somewhere in the depths of her monster-sized handbag, and they had to dig through all her junk to find them before Amy could let herself inside. Mrs. Sutton came home while Amy was getting her pills and wanted to talk to them about the upcoming weekend. And even when they were on the road, nothing went right. They got lost twice. Traffic was terrible. It seemed that everyone was heading up to the mountains for the weekend. "It's no good," Jessica declared. "We're not going to make it on time for me to talk to Liz before six-thirty," she moaned, turning off the highway to the exit for Mont Blanc.

"Well," Amy said philosophically, "you'll just have to save the day yourself, Jess."

"What do you mean?" Jessica demanded.

"Meet Jeffrey yourself and pretend you're Liz," Amy told her. "We should just make it to the lodge by six-thirty. If you hurry, he'll never have time to worry about where Liz is."

Jessica gripped the wheel tightly. "That's not a bad idea," she admitted. "It's kind of desperate, but I guess I'm in a desperate situation. I guess I can explain the whole thing to Liz as soon as I see her."

"See? Nothing's as bad as it seems," Amy said blithely, settling back to admire the gorgeous scenery as the jagged mountains rose around them. The peaks were snow-capped, and at that high altitude the air was as clear and cold as crystal.

Jessica smiled at her friend's complacent attitude. It *was* gorgeous up here, though, and she couldn't wait for the carnival to start.

She was just going to have to try her hardest to patch things up with Jeffrey herself—pretending to be her twin. She couldn't see any other way to avert disaster.

Fourteen

It was dark by the time Jessica pulled the Fiat into the small lot next to the Mont Blanc Inn. Shadows from the enormous trees fell across the snow, and the air outside the car was cold and crisp. "Mmm," Amy said, jumping out of the car and taking a deep breath. "Smell the pine, Jess!"

Jessica blinked and looked around her. The lights from the inn bathed everything in a soft bluish glow, and her eyes shone as she regarded the soft fir trees laden with glistening white and the Swiss-style lodge, looking warm and inviting before them.

"Why don't you go ahead and take your

stuff in?" Jessica said, seeing that the buses were parked in the lot. "The others are obviously all here already. If you go ahead and check us both in, I can go meet Jeffrey." Each student was supposed to check in with the head chaperon on his or her floor and go over the rules for the weekend before receiving a room key.

Amy was tugging on her suitcase, a helpless expression on her face. "OK," she grunted, finally heaving it out of the trunk. Amy and Jessica were going to share a room with Lila and Cara. The girls were staying in the main building of the inn, and the boys were staying in the lodge, about a hundred yards away.

"It's freezing out here." Jessica said, reaching in the trunk for her down jacket and zipping it up quickly. "OK, wish me luck."

"Good luck," Amy said, still wrestling with her suitcase.

Jessica hurried off, wondering what time it was and whether or not Jeffrey would be waiting for her at the lodge. She ran her fingers through her hair in an effort to comb it out, hoping she could stay in the shadows the whole time. She knew she wasn't wearing a particularly Elizabeth-like outfit. A hot pink sweater and white leather boots weren't the type of an outfit her sister would wear. Well, she thought, the jacket would cover the sweater, but there was nothing she could do about the boots. She'd just have to rely on her theatrical skill. Luckily she had had a lot of experience masquerading as her twin in the past and was used to acting the part under pressure. Although this whole thing seemed to be backfiring, Jessica thought she'd be able to do some fast talking to convince her twin this was all in her best interest.

Then she spotted Jeffrey, and there was no time to worry. It was time to be a good actress, and all other considerations had to be forgotten.

"Liz!" Jeffrey called in a low voice, stepping forward from the side door of the lodge. He looked serious, but not unfriendly.

"Hi," Jessica said, trying to sound shy and apologetic. "I'm really glad you came," she added. "I'm glad you weren't too angry to show up."

"Liz, I feel terrible about everything," Jeffrey said. "I've completely overreacted. I've been an overpossessive creep. I've—"

"I'm the one who's sorry," Jessica said softly. "I should have explained why I didn't meet you at the canyon. It was my sister's fault," she said self-righteously. "She had the car out too late, so I couldn't come meet you. I wanted to, but Jess made it impossible."

"You ought to punish that sister of yours," Jeffrey grumbled. Jessica didn't like this remark very much but didn't see how she could defend herself without blowing her cover.

"Just as long as you're not still furious with me," Jessica said hastily, looking uneasily down at his hand on her arm. She wanted to cut this short. There were a few guys hanging out on the steps of the lodge, and she didn't want anyone to see them together. She pulled back farther into the shadows, but Jeffrey moved even closer, staring at her with an intensity that alarmed her.

"I have to go back and get ready," she murmured. "Enid's waiting for me, and I—"

"So will you be my date this weekend?" Jeffrey asked, putting both hands on her shoulders and staring deep in her eyes.

Jessica blinked. "Uh—yes. Yes, of course," she said, trying to keep her voice tender. She would be enjoying this much more if it weren't taking place in so dangerously visible a location. In fact, she *really* wanted the conversation to end now. Chrissy Nolan, a senior who was known to be a gossip, was coming straight toward them. If they didn't hurry up . . .

"I'm glad everything's going to be all right," Jeffrey was saying tenderly, giving her a look of adoration that made Jessica feel very uncomfortable. If only he'd cut the mushy stuff, she thought, and let her go back to the lodge! And Chrissy was getting nearer every second.

"Well, I *really* should be heading back to the inn," Jessica repeated. "I'll meet you in a little while at the party, OK?" She pulled away with difficulty and turned to flee, but it was too late. Heading back to the inn, Chrissy had passed them and had surveyed them with great curiosity.

Great, Jessica thought, giving Jeffrey a weak smile as she hastened toward the inn. She wasn't sure how things had gotten so incredibly complicated. All she had wanted to do was to smooth things over between Jeffrey and Elizabeth. Now she couldn't tell whether she was succeeding or not. It seemed that she had, but then why was everything all tangled up all of a sudden?

She wasn't sure. But something told her

she'd better find Elizabeth—and the sooner
the better!

Elizabeth couldn't believe the frenetic
atmosphere of the second floor of the inn.
Dozens of girls were rushing from one room to
the next, borrowing perfume, exchanging
makeup or clothes, or gossiping with each
other. Radios blared from most rooms and
high-pitched, excited voices could be heard
everywhere. Each floor of the inn had two faculty chaperons, and the second floor, where
Elizabeth and Enid were sharing a room with
Olivia and Regina, had Ms. Dalton at one end
and Ms. Howard, a math teacher, at the other.
Despite her low spirits, Elizabeth was affected
by the atmosphere of silliness and excitement.
It was so much fun to be away from home for
the weekend, and the inn seemed almost like
a college dorm—or like Elizabeth's idea of one.
The small, cozy room the four girls were
sharing was filled with suitcases and ski
equipment. Elizabeth could barely turn
around.

"Hey, does anyone in here have any mascara to spare? I can't find mine," Chrissy
Nolan said, sticking her head in the room and

looking around with an inquisitive smile. Chrissy was in the room next door with three other seniors.

"I have some," Elizabeth said, reaching for her makeup bag.

"Thanks a lot," Chrissy said, looking strangely at her as she took the silver tube. "How did you get back so fast? I thought you were behind me on the path."

"What do you mean?" Elizabeth asked, confused.

"You know, down by the lodge a few minutes ago. You were with your boyfriend."

Elizabeth stared at her. "I haven't been anywhere," she said. "Not since we got up here an hour ago. You're sure it was me you saw?"

Chrissy laughed. "I guess I made a mistake. You have a twin, right? I always get you two confused. Come to think of it, she was wearing different clothes. And *she's* the one who goes out with that guy, isn't she?" She leaned forward to apply mascara to her lashes as she inspected her reflection in the mirror above the dresser. "It looked like the change in altitude was really getting to them. I guess it's a good excuse up here to have to keep warm!"

Elizabeth felt her face getting hot. She had no idea Jessica had arrived! And Jessica and

Jeffrey together! Was it possible? Elizabeth couldn't believe what she had heard. She couldn't believe Jessica would do this to her. She and Jeffrey had barely even broken up with each other—and Jessica was already moving in on him!

She said nothing to Chrissy, however, and was incredibly relieved when Chrissy returned her mascara and left the room. Her eyes stinging with tears, Elizabeth began throwing her clothes back into her suitcase, not even bothering to fold them. Enid, who had overheard the exchange with Chrissy, watched with concern.

"Liz, what are you doing?" she asked. "You're not going to take what she said seriously, are you? Jess might not have been with Jeffrey, and if she was, they were probably talking about *you*."

Elizabeth glared. "I doubt that! You notice that Jessica didn't ever bother to tell me she had arrived. She just isn't wasting any time. Well, I'm not going to waste any time either. There's no way I'm going to hang around here and be humiliated all weekend, watching my own twin sister walk off with—" Tears spilled down her cheeks, and she dashed them away impatiently. "With my ex-boyfriend," she said miserably.

"Where are you going?" Enid wailed, watching her zip up her bag and fling it over her shoulder with determination.

"Home," Elizabeth declared, her chin set stubbornly. "I'm not kidding, Enid. There's no way I'm going to stick around here. I thought it would be OK, but it obviously isn't going to be."

"But you can't just leave!" Enid ran to the window, peering out. "It's dark, for one thing. And it's starting to snow. How are you going to get home at this hour?"

"I'm going to get someone to give me a ride to the bus station. And I'm going to take the first bus back to Sweet Valley," Elizabeth said calmly.

She didn't wait to hear Enid's next objection. It was almost seven o'clock, and she wanted to get going before she ran into Jeffrey—or Jessica.

It was humiliating enough just imagining the two of them together. If she were to run into them she didn't know what she'd do!

Taking a deep breath, Elizabeth headed down the hotel corridor, ignoring the chattering and giggling she heard as she walked toward Nora Dalton's room. She didn't know what to tell the teacher. Probably just fibbing and saying she felt sick would be the best bet. She knew she couldn't leave without checking out, and she didn't want Ms. Dalton to worry about her. Yes, saying she was feeling unwell would be the best thing, she decided. It wasn't even a lie, really. At that moment she felt terrible.

She could barely wait to get home. This was the worst day of her life, and she couldn't wait for it to be over.

Fifteen

Elizabeth couldn't remember feeling as forlorn as she did twenty minutes later, huddled alone on the small bench just inside the Mont Blanc bus station, her duffel bag at her feet. Ken Matthews had given her a ride from the inn and had tried to stay with her until the bus came, but Elizabeth was adamant. She wanted to be alone.

Now she wished she had let him stay. It was cold in the bus station, and she felt incredibly miserable. She kept shifting on the bench, trying to get comfortable. The thought of all her classmates getting ready for the opening party kept running through her mind. Soon they'd be having pizza and sodas in the big central dining hall in the inn. Elizabeth's stomach growled. She hadn't had anything to eat since lunch, and she was starving.

She still couldn't believe Jessica would sneak around behind her back with Jeffrey. Was that why she had "accidentally" helped cause so many problems between her and Jeffrey? That seemed farfetched, but Elizabeth was cold, hungry, and lonely—and willing to believe it. She had never been so angry with her twin in her life. "I wish she had never been born," she muttered furiously to herself, grabbing her duffel bag as she saw the last bus from Sweet Valley pull into the lot. Ticket in hand, she made her way outside to board it.

"Liz! What are you doing here?" a familiar voice exclaimed. In the next instant Elizabeth was engulfed in an enormous bear hug.

"Steven!" she cried, throwing her arms around his neck as if she never wanted to let go. Cara, who had climbed out of the bus just after Steven, looked at Elizabeth with surprise.

"Did you come to meet us? But how did you know we'd take the bus? Did you know Steve's car was in the shop?" she asked, perplexed.

161

"No, I didn't," Elizabeth said, disentangling herself and wiping her eyes. "I'm going home. That's why I'm here."

"Home!" Steven stared at her, his dark eyes worried. "What for? Didn't you just get up here?"

Elizabeth nodded, swallowing hard to keep back her tears. "But I can't stay," she mumbled. "Everything's all messed up, and I—"

"Can you tell us what happened?" Cara asked gently, pulling the fur hood off her head and looking at Elizabeth.

Elizabeth shook her head. "I really can't go into it," she said. "I just have to go home, that's all."

"But the roads are getting slippery," Steven objected. A light snow was falling, and everything around them was covered with a white film.

"I'll be in the bus. I'll be OK," Elizabeth protested.

The bus driver had disappeared inside the station for a cup of coffee and was coming back now, the styrofoam cup steaming in his hand. "Any of you planning on taking the seven-fifteen? If so, we're about to get this show on the road. I want to be back before the roads up here get nasty."

162

Elizabeth jumped. "I'm coming," she called after him, grabbing her duffel bag.

"Liz, please stay and explain what's wrong," Cara begged.

But Elizabeth refused to listen. Giving her brother a quick kiss on the cheek, she lugged her bag up the steps into the bus and disappeared inside. She could see them waiting in the lot for the bus to depart, talking anxiously to each other and peering up into the bus.

Elizabeth knew she had worried them, but she didn't care. All she wanted was to get home now and forget this entire dismal day.

It turned out that Elizabeth was the only passenger on the bus. "Why don't you come up here and keep me company?" the bus driver called as they pulled out of the lot. Elizabeth walked forward to the front of the bus, and sat obligingly on the seat in the first row.

"Beautiful out there, isn't it?" he said. The fir trees glistened with soft white snow, and the sky was luminous with moonlight. It really *was* pretty, Elizabeth thought. It reminded her of the little paperweight her father had given her when she was small, a glass globe that

163

filled with snow when it was shaken. Tears filled her eyes, and she brushed them away.

"My name's Hank," the bus driver said, handing her a tissue. "You're feeling kind of sad about something, aren't you?"

Elizabeth nodded miserably. "I had—well, I guess a kind of misunderstanding with my sister."

"Hmm," Hank said, turning the bus down the main road from the mountain. "Sisters can be hard to deal with sometimes."

Elizabeth was quiet for a minute. "She's my twin, too," she mused. "You'd think that would make it easier in some ways. Aren't twins supposed to have some kind of mental telepathy?"

"I don't know about that. But twin or not, I know it's hard getting along with people in your family sometimes," Hank mused.

Elizabeth was quiet, watching the snow fall. *I wonder what it would be like if Jessica and I weren't twins*, she thought. *If I were the only daughter, and Jessica had never been born.* She tried to feel some kind of shock or sorrow at the prospect, but instead it seemed to her that it would be wonderful. Imagine not having Jessica around to bug her all the time about borrowing things. Not having Jessica to mess up all her plans, to make promises and back out of them, to make life continually difficult. . . .

"Well, remember," Hank said several minutes later. "Blood is thicker than water, and even if she's hard to get along with at times, she's still your sister."

Elizabeth's eyes filled with tears. How many hundreds of times had she said that to herself? And look where it had gotten her.

No, she was sure it was time for something different now. She wasn't going to make up with Jessica. She wasn't going to let her sister convince her that it was all just a simple little misunderstanding, that she had never meant any harm. There was no way she would ever forgive her twin this time.

The Wakefield house was dark when the taxi pulled into the drive. "Thanks," Elizabeth mumbled, handing the driver some bills and making her way up the front walk. She was incredibly tired, she realized. Even more tired than hungry. All the events of the past week had exhausted her. She couldn't wait to get inside and go to bed.

Her parents hadn't left a note, as they didn't

expect the girls to be back until Sunday. Elizabeth sighed and looked around her at the dark, quiet house. For a moment she almost wished she had stayed at the inn. Taking a deep, quavering breath, she went into the kitchen and made herself a sandwich. She was about to eat it when the phone rang, sounding loud and shrill in the silence. Elizabeth jumped in surprise and walked over to the phone. She picked it up on the third ring.

"Liz? It's Jess," a breathless voice cried. "God, I've been calling and calling you! How long did that stupid bus take to get there?"

Dumbfounded, Elizabeth didn't say anything for a minute.

"Cara told me," Jessica added. There was a faint roar behind her, and she seemed to be fidgeting with the phone. "It's really noisy here. I'm in the corner of the dining hall and Winston—Winston, *cut it out!*"

"Jessica," Elizabeth said coldly, "I really don't want to listen to this."

Jessica seemed stunned for a minute. "Liz, I just can't believe you've gone home," she said rapidly. "When Cara told me she had seen you at the bus station—"

"Jess, I know everything," Elizabeth interrupted furiously. "I know all about you and

166

Jeffrey meeting at the lodge. You don't have to keep pretending with me anymore."

Jessica seemed shocked. "Jeffrey and me—but, Liz, that was only because I was supposed to be *you*. I was trying to figure out a way to get you guys back together, only—"

"I'm sure you were," Elizabeth cut in frostily. "Jess, I'm sick of hearing your excuses. So why don't you just forget all this?"

Jessica sounded as if she were crying. "Liz, I'm not just saying this! Honestly. I wanted to—"

Elizabeth cut her off, steeling herself against her sister's tactics. She wasn't going to fall for them this time, she told herself. It seemed as though all the hurt and resentment that had been building for the last few weeks were about to explode.

"Jessica, I've had enough of you!" she cried angrily, tears running down her cheeks. "I've had enough of your stupid excuses and promises, and I'm just not going to stand for it anymore! "Jessica Wakefield," she added passionately, "I wish I'd never *had* a sister!"

And without waiting for Jessica's response, Elizabeth slammed the phone down as hard as she could.

She didn't feel like eating her sandwich

now. She was crying so hard it was difficult to see straight, and she had to hang on to the banister as she dragged herself upstairs. Flinging herself down on her bed, she cried as if her heart were breaking.

Finally fatigue got the best of her, and she drifted off to sleep. It was heavy, fitful, unhappy slumber, filled with fragments of disturbing dreams. She was almost relieved when she heard the phone ring.

It was probably Jessica again, she told herself, her anger returning. Probably calling back with more ridiculous excuses. Steeling herself, she picked up the phone beside her bed and answered with an abrupt, unfriendly "Hello."

"Is this the Wakefield residence?" a gruff voice asked.

"Yes," Elizabeth said, surprised.

"This is the Sweet Valley Police," the man said. "We've had a serious accident on Route Seventeen, down from Mont Blanc. A car skidded out of control and we've identified—"

"Jessica!" Elizabeth cried, sitting straight up in panic.

"Jessica Wakefield? Blond, medium height, wearing a—"

"Where is she?" Elizabeth wailed. She

couldn't bear to hear him go on this way. "That's my sister. Where is she?"

"She's in the emergency room at Fowler Memorial Hospital," the policeman told her. "But you'd better prepare yourself for a shock. From the report I just got, they're afraid they might lose her."

Elizabeth dropped the phone, her fingers trembling violently. Jessica—in a car crash . . . coming down from the mountain to find *her*, no doubt!

She didn't have time to think now. Not even to panic. She had to find a way to get to the hospital—and she didn't have a second to lose!

Sixteen

Elizabeth's heart was hammering wildly. She ran outside without a jacket, clutching her handbag under her arm and fighting for self-control. All she could think was that this was all her fault. If she hadn't been so furious, if she hadn't shouted those recriminations on the telephone, Jessica would never have tried to drive back on the icy mountain roads. The thought of her sister sliding out of control in the tiny Fiat made Elizabeth feel sick. She was having a hard time breathing. It was dark outside, and colder than she remembered. Why hadn't she grabbed a jacket? Unthinkingly

Elizabeth hurried across the front lawn. There was a light on in the window next door. Maybe the neighbors would drive her to the hospital. If only she knew where her parents were! What if—

But she couldn't let herself think. Not now. To her surprise, a black Camaro was slowing down as it passed the house, the headlights making round yellow circles on the trees. "Liz!" a familiar voice called, and Todd Wilkins rolled down the window on the driver's side.

Elizabeth stared. What was Todd doing here? Why wasn't he at the banquet? Her throat aching with tears, she raced around to the passenger side and opened the door. "Todd, I'm so happy to see you," she cried, getting inside. "Jessica's in terrible trouble. Can you take me to the hospital?"

Todd turned pale. "What happened?" he asked, starting the car again without delay.

"She was in an accident," Elizabeth choked out. Suddenly she felt as though she might break down. "Oh, Todd, thank goodness you're here," she kept saying. "I had no idea how I was going to get to the hospital. The police just called, and my parents aren't even home, and Jess—"

"Take it easy," Todd said, giving her an alarmed look. "Liz, you're white as a sheet."

"I'm so scared," Elizabeth whispered. She was trembling violently, and it was hard to focus on the road before her. Every time she closed her eyes she had a terrible image of the red Fiat spinning on the ice, sliding off the steep mountain road, and colliding . . . with what? A tree? Had the car turned over? Was Jessica still conscious?

They were approaching the hospital now, and Elizabeth felt a wave of dizziness come over her. This just couldn't be happening. "Jessica," she whispered, too terrified to cry. What an idiot she had been! How could she have even dared to say that she wished her sister had never been born?

"Come on," Todd was saying, putting his arm around her. "Liz, I think you're in shock. Just lean against me. We'll get you some water as soon as we're inside."

Elizabeth couldn't answer. Everything blurred before her: the lights in the parking lot; the red letters spelling Emergency, which loomed larger as they walked toward the entrance; and the ambulance with its bubble-light spinning around and around, shooting rays of colored light across the cement. She had no idea what she would do without Todd to hold her up. If only Jeffrey were here! But Jeffrey—she couldn't think about Jeffrey now.

"We're trying to find out the status of a patient who was admitted to the emergency room a little while ago," Todd told the nurse who came toward them. "Her name is Jessica Wakefield. Is there any way we can find out where she is and if she's OK?"

Elizabeth's knees went wobbly when she saw the look the nurse gave them. "Just a minute. I'll get Dr. Davis," she said, alarmed. "You'd better have her sit down," she told Todd in a stage whisper. "Her parents are already here. It's pretty bad, I'm afraid."

Her parents? How had they gotten here already? Elizabeth's head ached. She had a vivid impression of a clean linoleum floor beneath her as she sank into the chair Todd offered her. The next thing she knew, Dr. Davis, the twins' pediatrician, was coming toward her with a clipboard in his hand. He looked much younger than Elizabeth remembered, and he was wearing strange, slightly magnifying eyeglasses. But Elizabeth barely noticed.

"Dr. Davis!" Elizabeth cried, jumping up and throwing her arms around him. "Where's Jess? Is she OK?"

Dr. Davis patted her back gently. "You're going to have to be very brave, Elizabeth," he said. "I want you to remember that you're going to have to be brave, for your parents' sake especially. Remember, hard as it's going to be for you, it's going to be even harder for them."

Elizabeth felt as though the floor were sliding out from under her.

"She's fainted!" she heard Todd say, from what seemed to be about a mile away. She could feel the hard floor beneath her, and something smelled sharp and terrible, like ammonia.

"She's coming to," Dr. Davis was saying. His face swam before her, large and concerned, and Elizabeth sat up with an effort to discover she was lying on a cot in a curtained-off part of the emergency room.

"Is she really dead?" she whispered.

Dr. Davis picked up her hand and squeezed it tightly. "I'm sorry, Liz," he said gently.

Elizabeth felt every word cut like a knife. "Did she—was she still conscious when they brought her here?" she gasped.

Dr. Davis nodded. "She kept saying your name," he said tenderly. "She loved you so much, Liz. She kept saying that. She kept saying, 'Tell Liz I love her and I'm sorry.' "

Elizabeth couldn't bear it. Tears streamed down her cheeks as she turned her head to the wall. "It can't be true, it just can't," she said over and over again.

"Liz, I'm going to give you a pill. I want you to take it, and I want you to drink this," Dr. Davis was saying firmly, putting a small capsule in her hand. Elizabeth swallowed it obediently and drank the sweet liquid without question. "It's a tranquilizer. It's going to calm you down a little," Dr. Davis said.

"Did she suffer?" Elizabeth cried, anguished.

Dr. Davis shook his head sadly. "We did everything we could for her, Liz. We tried our hardest. The car smashed into a tree, and the impact was so . . . but no, I don't think she was in great pain. She was much more concerned about you than herself."

Elizabeth felt as if her tears were choking her. "It's all my fault!" she cried out, trembling again. "She wouldn't even have been in the car tonight if I hadn't been so selfish! I—"

"Liz, you need to try to rest," Dr. Davis said

175

firmly, pushing her back until her head was resting on the tiny pillow. "Try not to think," he advised her. "Todd and I will be right here when you wake up, Liz. I promise. We won't go away."

Elizabeth looked around her sister's room with a mixture of misery and disbelief. It looked exactly the way it always did. Clothes were strewn everywhere. Records, books, magazines, tags from new clothes, makeup, framed photographs—all the usual junk all over the place. Sinking down on her knees, Elizabeth stared disconsolately at her sister's belongings. Jessica was gone—really gone. What would they do with her room? Would they leave everything? Get rid of it all?

The door behind her opened then, and Mrs. Wakefield entered, her face terribly pale. There were dark shadows beneath her eyes. "Oh, Liz," she said brokenly. The next minute mother and daughter were in each other's arms, both in tears.

"Mom, I can't believe it. I just can't believe it," Elizabeth gasped, sobbing against her. "Is she really gone? Is it really true?"

"I can't believe it either," Mrs. Wakefield

said. "Your sister was so full of life, Liz. It's hard to imagine . . . it's impossible to imagine!" Her eyes were swollen, and she looked tenderly at Elizabeth as she brushed back her daughter's hair. "I know what you must be going through, honey. Much as your father and I are suffering, we know this is going to be hardest on you. She was part of everything you did—part of *you*." The next minute Mrs. Wakefield was sobbing. "I don't know how any of us is going to survive," she said brokenly. "We just aren't a family without Jessica!"

Despondent, Elizabeth sat down on the floor. She was holding one of Jessica's framed cheerleading pictures in her hands, and she stared down at it. She felt dizzy again, as if she might faint. "Mom, I don't feel very good," she whispered. Her heart was pounding like mad.

Mrs. Wakefield looked at her in alarm. "You've had a terrible shock," she said quickly. "Dr. Davis is really worried about your nerves. He wants you to keep taking these tablets until—" Her voice broke off, but Elizabeth could guess what the end of her sentence would have been.

Until she got used to it, she thought dully.

Until she got used to not having Jessica around. Until it seemed natural for Jessica's room to be empty, for the house to be quiet instead of filled with her laughter and chatter. Until she got used to being just Elizabeth, instead of one of the Wakefield twins.

Elizabeth's heart was breaking. She took the pill and glass of water her mother handed her. Reluctantly she swallowed the pill. Jessica's death was her fault. How could she take pills to subdue her grief? She was going to live the rest of her life with the knowledge that she had killed her twin sister.

Numbly she let her mother lead her downstairs, where her father was sitting in a daze, a stubbed-out cigarette in an ashtray before him. Elizabeth had never seen her father smoke before. She had never seen him look like this, either—so pale and haggard. Steven was sitting across from him, his head in his hands. They looked up briefly when Elizabeth entered the room.

Elizabeth realized from the pained expression in their eyes what they were thinking. *It hurts them to look at me*, she thought, horrified. *They look at me, and they remember Jessica.*

Her knees felt weak again as she sat down.

178

They'll never really be able to look at me again with-out thinking of her, she thought, miserable.

"You all think it's my fault!" she cried. "You all think I killed her!"

Her cry was greeted by silence. Her father turned and stared at her, and Elizabeth felt herself go cold all over. She knew she would never forget the accusing look in his eyes.

"We don't think that, Liz," Steven said quietly. "We know there's no point in accusing you. It was an accident. The argument you and Jessica had doesn't make any difference."

"Well, it makes a big difference to me," Elizabeth cried. "Do you realize how terrible I feel? If we hadn't quarreled she never would have tried to drive home. And she'd still be up at the ski lodge, instead of—"

"Liz, honey, please try to be calm," Mrs. Wakefield said. "Ned, she needs rest," she murmured in a low voice to Mr. Wakefield.

Mr. Wakefield didn't answer. He just kept staring dully at Elizabeth, a look of such utter grief and misery on his face that Elizabeth could barely stand his gaze.

The medication was starting to take effect, and the room began to blur a little. Elizabeth didn't care anymore. She just wanted to forget

179

everything—to let darkness wash over her and dreams intervene. And she dropped her head back against the sofa, tears streaming from behind closed lashes as she waited for sleep to blot everything out.

Seventeen

"Liz, don't you remember? Some of your friends are meeting at Enid's tonight to be with you and Steven." Mrs. Wakefield looked at Elizabeth penetratingly. "Aren't you going to get ready to go?"

Elizabeth *didn't* remember, but her mother was looking at her with such concern that she couldn't admit it. "Oh, yeah," she said, sitting up and blinking sleepily at Mrs. Wakefield. Her mother looked terrible. Her face was so pale, and she looked years older. And her eyes were red from crying. Strangely enough, the black skirt she was wearing belonged to Jessica. And she was wearing the same sweater that had provoked the argument between Jessica and Elizabeth days earlier. Elizabeth almost asked her why, but thought better of it.

"It's been a terrible week," her mother said sadly, looking past Elizabeth and out her bedroom window. "I keep thinking it will sink in, but it really hasn't. It's like being numb all the time, and every once in a while—for one horrible second—the pain comes back."

Elizabeth stared at her. "I know how you feel," she said in a low voice. So far she had been unable to tell anyone how she felt about Jessica. It was too horrible to put into words. All she could do was keep herself going, somehow, mostly by trying not to think about what had happened.

"We've changed her room, you know," her mother said. "Maybe you'd better go in and look." Elizabeth swallowed nervously. She felt that she couldn't bear to, but maybe her mother was right. "Come on. I'll come with you," her mother said, leading her down the hall.

Elizabeth opened the door and gasped. The room was completely changed! The chocolate-brown walls had been painted white. There were new curtains on the windows and a new carpet on the floor. Everything was spotless. None of Jessica's things were visible. The bed was neatly made, too. "We're going to use it for a guest room," Mrs. Wakefield said, looking around sadly. "It certainly looks different now, doesn't it?"

Elizabeth nodded. She was too miserable to say a word.

Now, listening to her mother's voice, she remembered about tonight. Enid had decided that something had to be done. The entire school had been in shock since the accident, but students had not been able to express their grief to one another. It was Enid's idea to have a small get-together—not really a memorial for Jessica, but a chance for Jessica's brother, sister, and closest friends to spend an evening together, talking about Jessica and about how they had been feeling since the accident.

"What time is it?" Elizabeth asked her mother, rubbing her eyes. She knew she couldn't get out of going to Enid's. Her best friend was doing what she could, and Elizabeth had to make an effort to show how grateful she was.

"It's five o'clock," her mother told her.

Elizabeth sighed. It was time to get dressed and head over to Enid's. But did she really need to change? Funny, she didn't remember that she was wearing a shimmering navy-blue dress. She looked down at it with a frown. It seemed to be made out of the same fabric as Jessica's ski suit. Or was she just going crazy? Elizabeth shook her head to clear it.

It would be good to go to Enid's. She needed to see other people. She thought she must be cracking up! There was no one Elizabeth could confide in now, though Todd had extended his visit and was still at the Egberts', and he had come by once or twice. Nice as it was to have his support, it was Jeffrey she needed. Only she wouldn't let herself see him. The very thought of Jeffrey brought her to tears. The whole terrible sequence of memories came flooding back— Jeffrey and Jessica by the lodge . . . the bus ride home . . . the awful phone call from the police. . . . Elizabeth sighed and pulled a brush through her hair. She couldn't imagine ever feeling like herself again. Dr. Davis said it would take time. How much time? How long before she could think of *anything* without thinking of Jessica? Without feeling as though all she wanted to do was to collapse in her mother's arms and cry her heart out?

Elizabeth had no idea, but her guess was

that this pain would never go away. "Give it time," Dr. Davis had said—but she had a feeling it was going to take more than time. It was going to take a miracle.

The group that had gathered at Enid's house was small and subdued. Only about ten close friends had been invited, as Enid sensed neither Steven nor Elizabeth would want to face a whole bunch of people. Cara had come with Steven; Winston and Todd were there; Amy Sutton and Lila Fowler, Regina Morrow and Bruce Patman, Olivia Davidson and her boyfriend, Roger Patman. They were all sitting in the Rollinses' living room, listening to records and talking in low voices.

"I hope it wasn't too hard for you to come tonight," Enid said softly to Elizabeth. "We've all been so worried about you, Liz. If there's anything we can do . . ."

"I just wish I could talk about it," Elizabeth said. "Dr. Davis keeps telling me that talking about it will make it easier, but I just can't."

"Well, you know we're here if you need us," Olivia said gently, patting her on the shoulder. "I guess that's all that matters, right?"

Elizabeth swallowed. "You're all such good friends," she said gratefully. "I just wish—"

"Oh, no. That's the door bell," Enid said, getting to her feet. "I wonder who it could be? Everyone's here already."

Elizabeth was pulling her fingers through the shag rug on the floor, her mind a million miles away. Todd was sitting next to her, but they weren't talking—they were just sitting in companionable silence—a silence that was suddenly and violently shattered when Jeffrey French walked into the room.

"Jeffrey!" Olivia exclaimed, giving Elizabeth an anxious glance. "Why don't you come in the kitchen for a second," she suggested, jumping to her feet and putting her hand on his arm.

But Jeffrey was staring down at Elizabeth, his eyes filling with tears. "Are you OK?" he whispered, dropping down and lifting her chin up so he could look at her face. "I've been worried sick about you," he added. The room was quiet. Everyone was keenly aware that this was the first time Jeffrey and Todd had met. And Elizabeth—how would Elizabeth react? She had made it clear that she didn't want to see Jeffrey again.

But Elizabeth seemed calm. Lifting her eyes

with apparent effort, she stared straight up at him. "It's good to see you," she said with effort, her eyes filling with tears.

Jeffrey sank down on his knees, pulling her head to his shoulder. "You poor thing," he said, stroking the back of her head gently. "You poor, poor thing."

The next minute Jeffrey's gaze fell on Todd, who was watching the reunion impassively. "You don't need to stare, Wilkins," Jeffrey said roughly.

"What do you mean? I'm not staring!" Todd exclaimed. A nervous hush fell over the room. Elizabeth pulled back and looked at Jeffrey.

"He isn't doing anything wrong—" she began. But Jeffrey was in no mood to listen.

"Look, haven't you caused enough trouble around here as it is?" he continued.

Todd went pale, then red. "What's that supposed to mean?" he demanded.

"You know what it means," Jeffrey said fiercely. "If it hadn't been for you . . ."

"Go on. Finish what you were going to say," Todd said. "If it hadn't been for me, what would have been different?"

"All I know is that two weeks ago everything was just fine around here. Then you showed up and started moving in on Liz, and all hell broke loose."

"I wasn't moving in on Liz," Todd insisted. The rest of the group looked around nervously at one another. No one knew exactly what to do or say. "Liz and I are old friends. I just wanted to spend a little time with her, that's all," Todd added defensively.

"If you hadn't started trouble between Liz and me, she and Jessica never would have gotten in an argument. And the accident would never have happened," Jeffrey said accusingly.

Elizabeth covered her ears with her hands. "Stop it!" she screamed. "Jeffrey, don't you see what you're doing to me?"

The tension in the room increased. Todd was clenching his fists, a murderous expression on his face. But Jeffrey refused to back down. "Why don't we go outside and take care of this—just you and me," he said, his eyes flashing. "I don't see much point in dragging anyone else into this. And I don't want Liz to be hurt, watching me kill you."

Elizabeth paled. "Jeffrey, *please*—I don't want you to fight with Todd! Haven't enough people been hurt as it is?"

Jeffrey's expression was violent. "What do

you say, Wilkins? Are you going to come outside with me and settle this for good, or are you going to sit in here like a coward?"

Todd jumped to his feet, his face pale. "All right, Jeffrey. We'll have it your way. To tell you the truth I've been dying to take a punch at you ever since I got back to Sweet Valley."

"Stop it, both of you!" Elizabeth wailed. "I can't stand it!"

But it was too late. There was no stopping either of them. Todd was shucking off his sweater, and Jeffrey was rolling his sleeves up. Then he stormed outside, and Todd followed him, smashing his fist over and over again into his own palm. Elizabeth felt sick. She couldn't believe this was happening.

"What am I going to do?" she asked Enid.

"Come on. We have to follow them to make sure they're OK," Steven said. "Enid, stay here with Liz," he commanded.

But Elizabeth refused to stay inside. "I've got to stop them," she kept saying brokenly. "I can't let them fight."

"You're not going anywhere," Enid cried, holding her back. "Cara, help me!"

Elizabeth broke free and rushed out through the front hall to the porch. Jeffrey was just tak-

189

ing a swing at Todd. Todd ducked, and Jeffrey lost his balance.

"I'm going to get you, Wilkins," Jeffrey grunted, grabbing him by the collar. Elizabeth blinked. What was going on? Why had Enid come running out—dressed in Jessica's silver ski suit?

"Leave him alone!" Elizabeth shouted. A low rumble filled the air, and she dragged her hand across her eyes, confused. She thought she heard someone calling her name— probably Enid or Cara—but she wouldn't turn around. It didn't sound like Enid or Cara, though.

First there had been the unmistakable sound of a car in the driveway. Headlights ran across the bed and the wall, but what was she doing in bed? Where was Jeffrey? And then she heard the garage door opening and the sound of rapid footsteps downstairs. Some- one was calling her name.

Elizabeth sat up with an effort. Her right arm was asleep, and her mouth was dry. She was upstairs, and the room was dark. Was that Jeffrey calling her?

"Liz? Where are you?"

"I'm up here," she croaked. She got up with an effort, noticing that her phosphorescent

190

alarm clock read ten-thirty. When had she fallen asleep? When had everyone left Enid's?

"Jeffrey?" she called, hurrying down the stairs and turning on the lights. Jeffrey was standing at the foot of the stairs, looking up at her with concern.

"Thank God you're here," a familiar voice said. "Jeffrey's been driving for *hours*. Those roads are like ice up on the mountain! Liz," she added, "you'd better forgive me now. After we put so much effort into coming back tonight to see how you are—"

"Jessica?" Elizabeth whispered, staring.

"Who'd you expect, the tooth fairy or something?" Jessica laughed.

"Jessica!" Elizabeth screamed. The next minute she was racing down the last few steps and throwing her arms around her sister. "You're alive!" she shouted, dancing around with her. "Jess, I've just been dreaming! You didn't crash after all!"

"Hey," Jessica said, laughing. Cara and Steven had just come into the hallway and were watching the scene with obvious interest. "It looks like she isn't mad at me anymore," Jessica called to them. "How do you think I managed that so easily?"

Elizabeth was laughing and crying at the

same time. "You're *real*. It's really and truly you!" she kept shrieking. She was so excited she had to hug Jeffrey, too. "And you're not fighting with Todd," she added happily.

"I'm not *what*?" Jeffrey asked, staring at her.

"Never mind," Elizabeth said, shaking her head. "I'll explain in a minute."

For the time being, all she wanted to do was to hug her twin over and over again. "I'll never say I wish I don't have a sister again," she promised, squeezing Jessica so hard her twin groaned.

"I think it was better when she was mad at me," she wailed. "It was a little easier to breathe then."

"I don't know about anyone else, but I'm hungry," Steven said. "All this excitement is using up calories fast. Liz, have we got any sandwich stuff around?"

Elizabeth began to giggle. She was thinking about the sandwich she had made for herself a few hours ago. If she had known what a rough evening she was going to have, she probably would have eaten it!

She was famished. And she was only too happy to follow the rest of them into the kitchen. As long as Jessica—the real, live Jessica—was there for her, she was happy.

She wasn't going to let Jessica out of her sight for a long, long time, she told herself. And she had learned her lesson. It was one thing to get mad at her twin from time to time. But never again, not as long as she lived, would she wish that Jessica weren't around. It had taken an awful nightmare to make her realize how lucky she and Jessica were to have each other.

Eighteen

"Now, do me a favor. Humor your older brother and explain this mess from the very beginning," Steven said. They were all sitting in the living room, sandwiches, cold drinks, potato chips, and brownies heaped on the coffee table. Elizabeth couldn't believe how hungry she was.

"I feel like Rip Van Winkle," she joked. "As if I were asleep for years instead of just a few hours."

Jeffrey was holding her hand tightly, his smile full of warmth and concern. "Liz, you have no idea how terrified Jessica was when she found out you'd gone home! Talk about putting a damper on a pizza party! When Ken came back from taking you to the bus stop, everyone jumped on him. No one could believe he'd actually let you go."

"Whoa!" Steven laughed, putting up his hand. "This is already too far along for me. I want to know what happened. Liz, why did you leave Mont Blanc in the first place?"

Elizabeth blushed and exchanged glances with her twin. "It's kind of complicated," she said.

"Yeah," Jessica said, rushing to her defense. "Let's put it this way, Steve. Liz and I have been having a number of misunderstandings lately, most of them my fault."

"Most of them?" Elizabeth laughed.

"Well, I guess all of them were really my fault," Jessica admitted. "Everything I've done for the past week or two seems to have backfired. Somehow I seem to have gotten Liz and Jeffrey mad at each other, and—"

"Now, that wasn't all your fault," Jeffrey cut in, still holding Elizabeth's hand. "The two of us had something to do with that, too."

Jessica looked grateful. "Anyway, I guess I didn't exactly pour oil on troubled water, or however you say it. I really messed up on Tuesday. Jeffrey had left Liz this note saying to meet him at Las Palmas Canyon if she still wanted to talk about things. And she meant to go, but I didn't have the car back in time."

"So that really did happen," Jeffrey murmured. "Liz, you should have just called later and explained."

"I know." Elizabeth sighed. "But it was all such a mess by that point. I know I should have, though. If I had, this whole mess could have been avoided."

"Wait a minute," Steven interjected. "I want to get to the bottom of 'this whole mess.' Jessica brought the car back too late for you to meet Jeffrey on Tuesday. Then what?"

"Then I decided to patch things up on my own," Jessica said.

"Uh-oh," Steven said with a grin. "I guess this was where things really fell apart, right?"

Jessica looked defensive. "I was only trying to help! It was obvious Jeffrey and Elizabeth were too stubborn to make up without some assistance, so I just thought I'd try to help them."

"Thanks," Elizabeth said dryly.

"Wait," Steven said, intrigued. "Can I just ask what form this 'assistance' took, Jess?"

Jessica helped herself to a brownie. "All I wanted was for Jeffrey and Liz to spend the evening together tonight. So I kind of forged a note to Jeffrey from Liz, saying that it was all off with Todd and she would meet him tonight at the ski lodge at six-thirty. See, I was going to explain everything to Liz on the bus ride up. Only Amy took forever getting ready, and we ended up missing the bus. There wasn't any time for me to find Liz before six-thirty."

A look of understanding came over Elizabeth's face. "So when you were talking to Jeffrey, you were pretending to be *me*?"

"What did you think I was doing?" Jessica demanded, outraged.

The whole room became quiet, and Elizabeth turned scarlet.

"You didn't think I was—" Jessica stared at her. "Liz, you can't be serious!"

Jeffrey was staring at her, too. "You mean you thought something was going on between Jessica and me?"

Elizabeth felt so embarrassed she could barely speak. "I—I didn't know," she stammered. "I mean, I was pretty sure that you wouldn't . . . that Jess wouldn't . . . but then when Chrissy Nolan came and told me she'd seen you two together and everything . . ."

Jeffrey looked horrified. "I had no idea that

197

was why you left Mont Blanc! Liz, how could you even think such a thing?"

Elizabeth looked at the expression on his face and couldn't suppress a giggle. "I guess I got a touch of jealousy myself," she admitted. "Kind of the way you were feeling about Todd and me."

Jeffrey reddened. "Good point," he said. "Liz, we've both acted like a couple of real idiots, haven't we?"

Elizabeth shuddered. "If you knew how vivid my dream was," she murmured, staring first at Jeffrey, then at Jessica. "I must've fallen asleep right after I hung up on Jess. The house was really quiet. I don't know where Mom and Dad are . . ."

"They're at a party," Jessica chimed in. "They should be back soon."

"Well, anyway, I dreamed that I was sleeping, and then the phone rang and woke me. It was the police, and they said Jessica had been in a terrible accident, driving down from Mont Blanc. Jess, it was terrible. Dr. Davis was at the hospital, and he told me . . ." She shook her head, trying to clear the awful memory of the dream.

"Dr. Davis!" Jessica exclaimed. "Liz, he moved to Arizona last year!"

Elizabeth had forogtten that. "I thought there was something strange about it. But the whole dream felt so real. All the details were so clear—like Jessica's room . . ."

"Don't tell me," Jessica said curiously. "Was my room neat?"

Elizabeth's eyes filled with tears. She couldn't shake the memory of the dream. "Jess, you were gone—and I couldn't tell you how sorry I was," she said brokenly.

"Oh, you goof. It was only a dream!" Jessica exclaimed, jumping up and going over to the couch to put her arms around her sister. "See? Pinch me. I'm really here."

Elizabeth wiped the tears from her eyes. "It was so awful," she repeated. "Oh, Jess— thank heavens you really are OK! If anything ever happens to you . . ."

"We're studying dreams in psychology," Steven told his sister, "and yours sounds to me like a classic guilt dream. Didn't you say you hung up on Jessica?"

Elizabeth nodded remorsefully. "And I told her I wished I'd never had a sister," she added in a low voice.

"See!" Steven exclaimed, snapping his fingers. "Then you went upstairs and dreamed

199

you really *didn't* have a sister. Straight out of a textbook," he said with satisfaction.

"Well, textbook or not, it was the worst dream I've ever had," said Elizabeth. "Jess, I'm sorry I got so mad at you. Do you forgive me?"

"As long as you forgive *me*!" Jessica exclaimed. "I felt so awful tonight when you hung up on me! Liz, I promise from now on that I'll be really good about the car. And I won't borrow any of your clothes without asking, and I'll do the dishes when it's my turn, and I'll—"

"Hey, what have we walked in on?" Mr. Wakefield, overhearing his daughter's vows, laughed as he and Mrs. Wakefield entered the room. "Sounds too good to be true, Jess. Have we missed something?"

"What are you all doing here?" Mrs. Wakefield asked. "I thought you were supposed to be up at Mont Blanc. Is something wrong?"

They all looked at one another and burst out laughing. "No, Mom, nothing's wrong," Elizabeth told her, smiling. "Not now, anyway."

"We had a few little things to iron out, so we decided to wait and go up to the carnival tomorrow morning," Jessica added, winking at her twin.

Mr. and Mrs. Wakefield looked at each other. "It was so peculiar, coming in and seeing the five of you," Mrs. Wakefield said. "I thought I was dreaming."

Everyone broke up at that. "Did I say something funny?" Mrs. Wakefield asked her husband. "Or are we just missing something?"

"Never mind, Mom," Elizabeth gasped, wiping tears of merriment from her eyes. "I think we're all just glad that you're *not* dreaming!"

Elizabeth knew she was glad of that, at any rate. It felt wonderful to look around the living room and see the happy faces of the people she cared most about. She just didn't want the evening to end. All that really mattered was that they were all there together. They were all safe, and they were all friends again.

"Listen, I'll be by to pick you up tomorrow around nine o'clock," Jeffrey said. They were standing in front of the Wakefield house saying good night. "It's going to be a tight squeeze, fitting everyone in. We all came down in my car tonight, so I guess that means we're all going back up in it tomorrow."

"Mmmm," Elizabeth said, putting her arms around him. She couldn't wait for the carnival now that everything was all right between them again. She didn't care how crowded the car was!

"I should have known that note Jessica left couldn't have been from you," Jeffrey said seriously. "It was stupid of me. For one thing, her tone was different from yours. She seemed to brush off everything that had happened, and I know you would never do that. She said something about not caring about 'that dumb banquet.' And I guess I wanted to think that you would dismiss it that way, but if I had thought about it, I would have realized that wasn't the sort of thing you'd say."

"I felt terrible about the banquet," Elizabeth said seriously. "On the one hand I really would have preferred, right from the start, to go to the carnival with you. But I felt obligated to Todd as an old friend."

"You were right, too," Jeffrey told her. "I realize now what a fool I've been for the last week or two. Tonight, when I was afraid something might have happened to you when you took the bus back alone . . ." He shuddered. "I'm sorry about the way I behaved now, Liz. I was jealous of Todd. I didn't want anyone trying to take you away from me."

Elizabeth smiled gently at him. "I think Todd understands that. In fact, I have a feeling that that may have something to do with his sudden decision to go to the banquet alone tonight."

"Well, you said he's going up to the carnival tomorrow morning, too. If it's OK with you, I'd like to offer him a ride with us," Jeffrey said, "even if it will be really crowded."

Elizabeth's face lit up. "What a wonderful idea!" She threw her arms around him and hugged him tightly. "Have I mentioned lately how fond I am of you?" she said teasingly.

Jeffrey laughed. "Not recently, as a matter of fact. But now that you *have* mentioned it . . ." He lifted her chin and gazed tenderly into her eyes. "Let's not argue again," he said softly. "I love you, Elizabeth Wakefield."

Elizabeth felt a lump forming in her throat. "I love you too," she whispered.

The next minute Jeffrey had tightened his arms around her, and he was kissing her deeply. Elizabeth felt her heartbeat quicken. *This* was a dream she never wanted to wake up from, she thought happily.

Nineteen

"What took you guys so long? We've all been frantic about you!" Enid exclaimed, hurrying to meet the small group walking up the path to the lodge from the parking lot. Elizabeth and Jeffrey were heading the line and had their arms around each other. Jessica was next, talking animatedly to Todd, who had come in Jeffrey's car after all. Steven and Cara brought up the rear.

"We got a slow start this morning. Liz took forever getting ready," Jessica complained with a grin. She had phoned the lodge at Mont Blanc early that morning to tell Ms. Dalton that all of them, including Elizabeth, would be back as soon as possible.

Elizabeth scooped up a handful of snow. "Don't even *try* it, Jessica Wakefield!" she hollered, chasing her twin.

"Translation: Jessica overslept," Steven said with a chuckle. "Have we missed much this morning?"

"Just the best pancake breakfast ever," Enid declared. "We made them promise to make them again tomorrow morning for you guys, though. Come on, come on. The Winter Olympics are supposed to start in just a few minutes!"

Bright sunlight was shining over the mountainside, and the magic of the sparkling snow strongly affected the latecomers. "It's so beautiful up here!" Elizabeth gasped, her arm still around Jeffrey's waist. Diamond-bright snow glittered in the boughs of the dark green fir trees. There was snow everywhere—brilliant, glistening snow that Todd and Steven declared was perfect "packing"—ideal for snowball fights. Though it was only eleven o'clock in the morning, the mountaintop had already been transformed by the swarm of juniors and seniors. A snowy meadow was the site of a snowman-building contest. A group of seniors was rolling a ball bigger than anything Elizabeth had ever seen. "We're making the world's biggest snowman!" Bruce Patman called as they strolled past. "Come join us!"

But that was only one of the many events that was already under way. Amy Sutton was running the ice show at the outdoor rink next to the meadow, and Jessica ran off to join her, leaving her luggage for Elizabeth to take up to the lodge.

"Good old Jess has recovered from worrying about me." Elizabeth passed one of her sister's bags to Jeffrey. Secretly she didn't mind. It wasn't such a big deal to take her sister's things for her. And Jessica was Jessica; that was all there was to it.

"She's trying to score points for the Blue Team," Cara confided. "It's the old competitive streak. You know Jess just wants to make sure she walks off with a victory."

"I want to go tobogganing," Jeffrey said. "Liz, should we get rid of all this stuff and hit the slopes?"

"I'd love to!" Elizabeth declared. She looked shyly at Todd, waiting for a minute.

But Jeffrey, sensing how she felt, took the

initiative. "Todd, want to join us?" he asked casually.

Todd grinned. "I'd love to. How about if I introduce you to one of the great pastimes in Vermont?"

"What's that?" Elizabeth asked, intrigued.

"It's perfectly simple. All we need are a few lids from some garbage cans—I see some over there near the lodge—and a lot of nerve. Let's put those bags away, and I'll show you!"

"I can't remember ever having so much fun!" Enid exclaimed. It was late afternoon, and she and Elizabeth were sharing a quick cup of hot chocolate at the lodge beside the crackling fire before going out to watch the end of the contests. Todd and Jeffrey were competing together for the Red Team in the final event, the cross-country ski relay, and the girls wanted to warm up before watching the long competition.

For Elizabeth it had been a wonderful day. The sky was bright blue and cloudless, and the crisp air made everyone's cheeks bloom with color. Everyone was in a good mood, and high spirits seemed to be infectious. Mr. Collins and Ms. Dalton had helped the seniors decorate the massive snowman they'd built with stray bits of clothing. By the time they were finished, everyone agreed it looked an awful lot like Chrome Dome Cooper, the principal of Sweet Valley High. Next, everyone had to have pictures taken with the snowman. The silliness seemed endless.

The ice show quickly lost its organized perfection and turned into frenetic ice-dancing, with loud rock tunes blaring from the PA system. Most of the outdoor sports had similarly become more creative than competitive, but the students had been keeping careful track of points. There were four teams, Blue, Red, Yellow, and White, which had been formed earlier. Every event that weekend was judged by one of the faculty members. On Sunday afternoon one of the teams would be announced the winner. But scoring points didn't seem to be half as important as having a good time. Todd's trash-can-lid tobogganing proved to be the hit of the afternoon, as student after student sailed down the mountainside, screaming and clinging to the side of the lid as it whizzed at breakneck speed down to the level plateau hundreds of feet below.

All this exercise made everyone hungry, and a hearty lunch of chili and hot dogs helped warm the group in preparation for the long afternoon. A spontaneous snowball fight had erupted after lunch, and by the time everyone had calmed down, it was time for more athletic events.

"What are you wearing tonight?" Elizabeth asked Enid as they put down their hot drinks and zipped their jackets up in preparation for the bracing cold air.

"My blue and white dress," Enid replied. "What about you?"

Elizabeth smiled mysteriously. "Something special," she said ambiguously. "I promised myself that I'd bring it up if everything got straightened out between Jeffrey and me. And this morning I took it out of the closet." She giggled at the look on her friend's face. "Don't worry. It's perfectly respectable," she promised. "It's just a fun dress, that's all." She knew how much work Enid and Winston had put into the dance, and she was sure it was going to be the highlight of a wonderful weekend.

"Come on! They're about to start!" Steven yelled when he saw Enid and Elizabeth. They quickly put on their gloves and hurried out to join all their classmates, who were in a huddle at the starting line. Elizabeth and Enid were both members of the Red Team and had a definite interest in the cross-country ski race. There were eight contestants in all—two from each team. Each team member had to ski half of the mile-long course. Todd was going to ski first and then pass a baton to Jeffrey, who would finish the course.

"Come on, Jeffrey and Todd!" Elizabeth screamed.

Bruce Patman was the official starter. "OK, guys," he called above the cheers of his schoolmates. "On your mark, get set—*go!*"

Pandemonium seemed to break out as the crowd moved along to a better viewing point. The course curved behind the lodge and came out again at the finish line, marked by a taut red tape. More people had come to watch this event than many of the others, since it was the last competition before the dance contest at the Snow Ball.

Elizabeth's heart beat wildly as they rounded the first bend. Aaron Dallas, one of the contestants from the Yellow Team, was in the lead! "Come on, Todd!" she screamed. Todd was in second place when he passed the baton to Jeffrey.

Jeffrey seemed to be edging closer to Bill Chase, who was Aaron's teammate. Then

Todd seemed to be edging closer to Aaron. Bill was still in the lead behind the lodge, but he seemed to be falling back. Then, just past the lodge, Jeffrey was in the lead, heading straight for the red tape!

The crowd went wild when Jeffrey sailed through, the tape breaking against his chest. "Jeffrey and Todd are the winners!" Bruce cried, and Elizabeth ran forward to hug Jeffrey, beside herself with joy. He and Todd patted each other on the back, and Elizabeth knew then that everything was fine between them.

"You're a terrific skier, Jeffrey," Todd said appreciatively, shaking his hand. "You should come out to Vermont and teach me a few tricks."

"You aren't half bad yourself." Jeffrey grinned. "And I'll take you up on the first part of that anyway." He looked at Todd with genuine warmth. "Nice being your partner," he said gruffly, slapping Todd on the back once more.

Elizabeth smiled as she watch them ski off together. "Enid, I've started a wonderful friendship. You think either of them will remember to ask me to dance tonight?"

"I think," Enid said, her green eyes twinkling, "that if you play your cards right and wear your special new dress, one or the other of them just might remember."

"Oh, Enid!" Elizabeth gasped, stepping forward with a look of astonished pleasure on her pretty face. She couldn't believe how beautiful the ballroom at the inn looked. It was like a sparkling snow palace.

Tinsel streamed from the beams overhead and was laced through the fir boughs decorating the windowsills and cornices. White crepe paper covered all the walls, so the whole room was white and silver. The Droids, Sweet Valley High's own rock band, had set up their instruments on a dais in one corner. The dais was covered with artificial snow, and the Droids were all dressed in white. They were playing a rock version of "Winter Wonderland" as couples streamed into the room.

A long table set up at one end of the room was filled with delicious-looking desserts— cakes with white icing, mounds of vanilla ice cream, and snow-white cookies—and a bowl of sparkling punch. It looked scrumptious, and the total effect was pure magic.

"The best is yet to come," Enid whispered to her friend.

Elizabeth barely heard her. Jeffrey had just come into the room, and she drifted toward him, keenly aware of the effect she was having. Jeffrey's mouth dropped open as he stared at her. He had never seen Elizabeth look so beautiful.

She had found the dress weeks before and couldn't decide whether to buy it at first. It was silver silk, with slightly puffy sleeves ending at the elbow, a round neck, and a soft full skirt. The fabric shimmered like ice. With a small strand of pearls around her neck and tiny silver and pearl earrings, Elizabeth felt wonderfully glamorous. And Jeffrey's expression told her the outfit was perfect.

"My God," he whispered, taking her by the arm. "Liz, you look . . ." His voice broke off.

"I took one look at it and thought only Jessica would buy something like this. So I bought it!" Elizabeth said and grinned.

The Droids were playing the opening notes of the song they had written especially for the evening, "Snow Girl."

"May I have this dance?" Jeffrey asked with a deep bow. In his white linen jacket and crisp white trousers, he looked extremely handsome, and Elizabeth's pulse quickened as he slipped his arms around her.

Dana Larson, the Droids' lead singer, sang the lyrics in a rich, throaty voice. "We live in such a cold world don't let it make us cold. You know you are my snow girl. You turn ice into gold . . ."

Couples were drifting out to the dance floor now. Elizabeth could see Jessica dancing with Ken Matthews and Enid dancing with Todd. Steven and Cara were coming out, too. Lila, wearing an extravagant dress with white feathers all over it, was dancing with a senior named Craig.

"I love you so much," Jeffrey whispered in Elizabeth's ear. Elizabeth tightened her arms around him. It was a magical dance—the start of a magical evening.

"You took my heart, girl, which was ice," Dana sang, closing her eyes. "One look from you and I'm on fire, so let's just listen to our hearts, girl. Lift our hearts up even higher . . ."

Elizabeth sighed in utter contentment. Mr. Collins was leading Ms. Dalton out on the dance floor now, and applause broke out as Winston ran out to the center of the dance floor and released dozens of silver and white helium balloons. They floated up to the ceiling, shimmering and bouncing, and the applause swelled.

Elizabeth looked up at Jeffrey with utter joy. And beside her, Jessica was dancing with Ken—close enough so Elizabeth could reach out and touch her and prove to herself that she was really there.

She knew she would never ever regret having a twin again.

□ 25789-7 **JUST ANOTHER DAY IN PARADISE,**
Maxwell $2.95

Fiddler has more money than he knows what to do with, he's tried about everything he'd ever thought of trying and there's not much left that interests him. So, when his ex-wife's twin brother disappears, when the feds begin to investigate the high-tech computer company the twin owns, and when Fiddler finds himself holding an envelope of Russian-cut diamonds, he decides to get involved. Is his ex-wife's twin selling high-tech information to the Russians?

□ 25809-5 **THE UNORTHODOX MURDER OF
RABBI WAHL,** Telushkin $2.95

Rabbi Daniel Winter, the young host of the radio talk show "Religion and You," invites three guests to discuss "Feminism and Religion." He certainly expects that the three women, including Rabbi Myra Wahl, are likely to generate some sparks . . . What he doesn't expect is murder.

□ 25717-X **THE BACK-DOOR MAN,** Kantner $2.95

Ben Perkins doesn't look for trouble, but he isn't the kind of guy who looks the other way when something comes along to spark his interest. In this case, it's a wealthy widow who's a victim of embezzlement and the gold American Express card she gives him for expenses. Ben thinks it should be fun; the other people after the missing money are out to change his mind.

□ 26061-8 **"B" IS FOR BURGLAR,** Grafton $3.50

"Kinsey is a refreshing heroine."—*Washington Post Book World*

"Kinsey Millhone . . . is a stand-out specimen of the new female operatives." —*Philadelphia Inquirer*

[Millhone is] "a tough cookie with a soft center, a gregarious loner." —*Newsweek*

What appears to be a routine missing persons case for private detective Kinsey Millhone turns into a dark tangle of arson, theft and murder.

Look for them at your bookstore or use the coupon below: